"Get behind

Another shot w ead.
He hunkered do

"There is no pla till
up there." Stewart pointed to where he thought the
shots had come from.

Lila rested her face in her hands. "Then what are you going to do? Wait him out?"

Now that he'd seen an attack firsthand, he was willing to admit that Lila's return had made someone very nervous. Had there been a third man involved in the robbery, and had he been living in this town the whole time? Or had he, too, returned when the new evidence had surfaced?

"Crawl straight out from the truck. And then make a run for those trees."

They moved slowly, both of them glancing over their shoulders. Stewart thought he saw a man hunkered down in the tall grass. Once the land flattened, Stewart and Lila rose and sprinted toward the trees just as another shot was fired.

Ever since she found the Nancy Drew books with the pink covers in her country school library, **Sharon Dunn** has loved mystery and suspense. Most of her books take place in Montana, where she lives with three nearly grown children and a hyper border collie. She lost her beloved husband of twenty-seven years to cancer in 2014. When she isn't writing, she loves to hike surrounded by God's beauty.

Books by Sharon Dunn

Love Inspired Suspense

Wilderness Target
Cold Case Justice
Mistaken Target
Fatal Vendetta
Big Sky Showdown
Hidden Away
In Too Deep
Wilderness Secrets
Mountain Captive
Undercover Threat
Alaskan Christmas Target
Undercover Mountain Pursuit
Crime Scene Cover-Up
Christmas Hostage
Montana Cold Case Conspiracy

Alaska K-9 Unit

Undercover Mission

Visit the Author Profile page at LoveInspired.com for more titles.

MONTANA COLD CASE CONSPIRACY

SHARON DUNN

LOVE INSPIRED SUSPENSE
INSPIRATIONAL ROMANCE

ISBN-13: 978-1-335-58848-7

Montana Cold Case Conspiracy

Love Inspired
22 Adelaide St. West, 41st Floor
Toronto, Ontario M5H 4E3, Canada
www.LoveInspired.com

Printed in U.S.A.

He that dwelleth in the secret place of the most High shall abide under the shadow of the Almighty. I will say of the Lord, He is my refuge and my fortress: my God; in him will I trust. Surely, he shall deliver thee from the snare of the fowler, and from the noisome pestilence. He shall cover thee with his feathers, and under his wings shalt thou trust: his truth shall be thy shield and buckler. Thou shalt not be afraid for the terror by night; nor for the arrow that flieth by day.

—*Psalm* 91:1–5

For my God who is my protector
and the giver of all good things.

ONE

The wipers of Lila Christie's rental car worked at a furious pace as rain slashed across the windshield. She leaned forward, straining to see the road. Out here in the country with no artificial light, objects were more shadow than substance. Because of the distortion created by the downpour, her headlights offered only a murky view of the gravel road ahead. From what she remembered, springtime in this part of Montana was always rainy.

Her car edged up a hill, gears grinding as the tires sunk down in the mud. Once at the top, she saw the fuzzy lights that indicated her destination, The Lazy DN Bar Ranch. Her breath caught. Ten years was a long time to be gone from here. Stewart Duncan, owner of the ranch, was the one man who might be able to help her, the one person who should care about new evidence surfacing in the bank robbery ten years ago. His father had been killed that day. Her father had fallen off the face of the earth. She could not let go of the belief that her father had been coerced into participating in the robbery of the bank where he was the manager. And that he was hiding somewhere. She would not give up hope until she found her father alive or his remains were located.

As she made her way down the muddy hill, the car jiggled and slipped into some ruts. Headlights filled the rearview mirror. Judging from how high up the lights were, the vehicle was bigger than her sedan. Was that guy actually trying to pass in these conditions? So dangerous. The road was only one lane at best. A tap on her bumper caused her car to jerk forward and then slide sideways. Lila gripped the wheel, trying to stay on the road while her heart pounded erratically.

The other vehicle plowed into her bumper a second time with such force that the seat belt dug into her skin, and she bit her tongue. Headlights surrounded her and invaded the cab of her car. She was being pushed off the road, and there was nothing she could do but hold on. After rolling forward from impact her car hit the side of a ditch with a jolt. The front end of the car slanted downward.

Lila struggled to take in a breath and process what had happened as the rain pelted her car. When she turned her head, she saw no sign of the vehicle that had run her off the road. She tried only once to shift into Reverse and back out. The wheels spun, and her car made a strange grinding noise. She was stuck.

She reached for her phone and dialed Stewart's number. Her voice trembled almost as badly as her hands. Voice mail came on inviting Lila to leave a message. She closed her eyes. "Stewart, this is Lila Christie. I left a message earlier that I was coming to see you. I assume you got it. It seems I am stuck in a ditch not too far from your place. Someone ran me off the road. I'm not sure what's going on here—"

A female voice came on the line. "Hello. Sorry, I was running for the phone. Who is this?"

Even after all these years, she recognized Stewart's mother's voice. "Mrs. Duncan." She couldn't bring herself to call her former art teacher by her first name. She took a deep breath. "This is Lila Christie."

"Lila Rose, my best student. To what do I owe the privilege?" Even over the phone Lila picked up on the tension in the older woman's voice.

"I'm trying reach Stewart. I left a message earlier. I'm back in town actually."

"Oh… I didn't realize." No doubt, Lila's presence reminded Mrs. Duncan of the tragedy that had taken her husband's life. Why someone as positive and kind as Cindy Duncan had stayed married to a violent cheat like Stewart Duncan Sr. had been a mystery to the whole town.

"My car is stuck in the mud not too far from the ranch. Some guy with road rage ran me into a ditch. I don't suppose Stewart could come pull me out." She pressed her lips together. This was a horrible way to return after not having any communication for so long.

"He could but he's not here. He's out looking for some wayward calf. He's probably left his phone in his truck if he took it at all. Randy Clarins up the road has a big truck and a winch. Let me give him a call."

"Thank you." Despite the logistical nature of the conversation she felt a heaviness between them. Just by returning, Lila was dredging up old history that most people in this area probably wanted to forget. "Forgive me for not staying in touch, and I'm sorry that the very first thing I do when I come back is ask for help."

Mrs. Duncan didn't answer right away. "Let's just work on getting you back on the road."

"Thank you."

"You sit tight now," said Mrs. Duncan. "Weather like this is not fit for man nor beast to be out in."

Lila pressed the disconnect button, releasing a pent-up breath. After removing her seat belt, she rested her head against the back of the seat. Had it been a mistake to come out here? She hadn't known where else to turn when she'd learned the getaway car had been found in another county. Apparently, it had been parked on a riverbed and partially covered by water all this time.

The news story had been brief, indicating that the police were being tight-lipped. It was a local story. She would not have seen it at all except she had Google alerts set up for any keyword that might bring up a story about the robbery.

Stewart was a sheriff now and had connections. She hoped that he could find out more than the newspapers were saying. She needed to know if there were human remains in or around the car. Maybe she had been impulsive in getting on a plane and coming here. Somehow she thought a face-to-face conversation would yield more than talking on the phone. Because of their history, Lila had been afraid that Stewart wouldn't even take her call. Before the robbery, they had been engaged to be married.

Maybe there had been no love lost between Stewart and his father, but he had to want to know who had killed him. Despite what everyone thought, she knew her father was not a killer or a thief. He had been a loving and kind man.

In the side-view mirror, she saw movement. Someone in a rain slicker and a hat was coming toward her. His head was down to protect from the rain. Maybe Stewart had found her, or it was the man his mother had mentioned? She opened the door a few inches and stuck her head out. “Hello. Did you come to help pull me out?”

The man said nothing. He stood about twenty feet from the car. He raised his hand. A strange explosive boom, almost drowned out by the rain, surrounded her. She slammed the door shut.

Had she just been shot at?

She fell across the seat. Her heart pounded and her mind reeled from fear. He was coming toward her on the driver’s-side door.

She stretched across the seat, pushed open the passenger door and crawled out. When she looked back through the window, she didn't see him anywhere. Rain stabbed at her skin as she crouched by the car.

The noise of a boot squishing in mud alerted her to the fact that the assailant was coming around to her side of the car.

Heart pounding, she moved toward the front of the car and knelt by the bumper. She turned sideways. The lights of the ranch were hidden by a hill, but she could guess at where it was. She had to make a run for it.

She took off at a sprint, racing through the tall prairie grass. Another shot was fired. Even in the downpour the sonic boom engulfed her. She gulped in air and kept running. The only thing moving faster than her feet were her thoughts.

What is happening here?

Heading in the general direction of the ranch, she prayed she would see the lights again. She'd be safe from the wild gunman if she could get there.

She slipped in the mud and reached her hands out to brace the fall. Something sharp cut her palm. Another shot was fired but not close to her. The shooter was having trouble seeing through the dark and sheets of rain.

She stayed on the ground for a moment longer trying to collect herself as rain soaked her clothes. Her hand stung where she must have landed on a sharp rock. Lila rose slowly, still bent over. She straightened and kept moving through the dark.

Strong arms reached out for her, pulled her close.

She screamed. The shooter had decided to eliminate her face-to-face. She lashed out, flailing her arms wildly.

"Whoa, whoa, whoa."

She knew that voice. Even after ten years, the warm tenor of Stewart Duncan's voice calmed her. She stilled.

"What's going on here?"

"I might ask you the same thing, Stewart," she said. "This is not the welcome home I had envisioned."

Stewart's voice filled with surprise. "Lila? What on earth..."

Clearly, he hadn't been expecting her.

"Someone ran me off the road and shot at me."

"I didn't hear any shots," he said.

"It was from a pistol. The rain was loud." Did he not believe her?

"You're soaking wet. Come this way." Stewart's arm curled around her waist as he all but carried her.

The trauma of the wreck and being shot at had taken its toll. She felt herself shutting down as Stewart lifted her into the cab of his truck. Rain spattered on his cowboy hat when he leaned close to her. "I've got a missing calf to find before she freezes to death." He got behind the wheel and glanced over at her. "Maybe you can tell me what is going on here?"

She wrapped her arms around herself and shivered. He must have sensed that she was in no condition to talk. His voice grew softer. "If I don't find this calf in the next five minutes, I'll take you back to the house and go out again."

He drove through the inky darkness. She could not measure how much time passed. She was grateful the heater was on full blast.

Stewart came to a stop and turned the steering wheel. "There we go, little one." His words took on a soothing quality as he peered through the windshield.

At the edge of the headlights' range, she could just make out the tiny calf huddled on the ground. He jumped out of the truck, leaving the engine running. Returning a moment later, he lifted the calf into the cab of the truck. "She's as cold as you are."

Lila placed her hand on the wet hide of the little creature. The rise and fall of the calf's breathing was somehow a comfort to her. They were both weak but still alive.

Once Stewart made it back to the gravel road, he increased his speed. As the lights of the ranch house and outbuildings came into view, she wondered again if coming back here was a mistake. Clearly her arrival had stirred up trouble about the past. That had to be why she had been shot at. But what she hadn't counted on was how the feelings for Stewart she thought were long dead rose up just by hearing his voice.

As he pulled up close to the house, Stewart Duncan's mind raced. Not a day had gone by that he hadn't thought that Lila might return and say that breaking their engagement ten years ago had been a mistake. Now that she was sitting in the cab of his truck, the moment felt surreal. He couldn't begin to process why she was being shot at or even if she had been. That level of violence didn't happen around here, not since the robbery their fathers had been a part of.

There would be time to sort through all of it. His priority right now was getting Lila and the calf warmed up.

He jumped out of the truck and reached back in for the shivering mass of hide. "I've got to get this calf inside. Can you walk to the house, or do you need me to come back for you?"

The way Lila stared at the floor suggested she was in shock. "I can make it."

He carried the calf up the stone walkway. The truck door slammed, and Lila caught up with him.

"I can get the door." Her voice was barely above a whisper. She twisted the knob and pushed it open.

"After you," he said.

He stepped in behind her. "Ma, I need your help." The lights in the living room were dim. His mother had to be in her studio.

Mrs. Duncan emerged from a back room. She took in the scene. "Three drowned rats. Hello, Lila. I see you made it. Randy wasn't home, and you didn't answer when I called you back."

Lila nodded. His mother's posture had a stiff quality. Her attempt at sounding welcoming felt a little strained.

"Let's get you out of those wet clothes and into a hot shower." His mother had not seemed overly surprised to see his ex-fiancée as she ushered Lila down a hallway. Stewart laid the calf beside the woodstove and rubbed its trembling body trying to bring some life back into the tiny creature.

His mom rushed into the living room and handed him three folded towels. He dried the calf with two of them and then placed the third one over it. He grabbed a throw from the sofa and covered the calf. The little one was alive but not terribly responsive.

Down the hallway, he could hear the shower running. His mother wore an oversize shirt stained with the evidence of past painting and sculpting projects.

"Quite a night for surprises, huh?" his mom said.

Stewart rose to his feet and sat down on the sofa. He nodded. "Lila says she was shot at."

"Oh, my. She called earlier. She said she'd been run off the road."

That explained why his mother wasn't surprised to see Lila.

"For someone who hasn't been back here for ten years that sort of response seems extreme. I'm going to call my deputy. See what he can find out."

Focusing on the logistics of the crime meant he didn't have to think about how Lila's return made him feel tangled up in knots. Maybe their love had just been too fragile to survive tragedy and unanswered questions. Though she had been the one to leave town, he had seen the cracks in the relationship after the robbery.

He made the call to the deputy on duty and asked him to have a look around where Lila had gone off the road.

His mom took a chair opposite Stewart. After hanging up the phone, he listened to the crackling of the fire in the woodstove.

"Her story sounds a little…out there," said Cindy Duncan. "Maybe run off the road, but being shot at?"

Stewart knew what his mother was thinking without giving details. Lila's mother had suffered from paranoid delusions even before the robbery. After the disappearance of her husband, Richard, Marian Christie had taken her own life.

"Lila isn't like her mom," said Stewart. Really, though, he didn't know what Lila was like. He hadn't seen her in ten years.

A chill came into his mom's voice. "Why is she back here after all this time?"

Stewart took off his wet cowboy hat and spun it around in his hands. "Not sure." He had a feeling, though, that it had something to do with the getaway vehicle being found. The sheriff's report from Lewis County had come across his desk in a pile of other crimes that might be of concern to him. The car had been concealed for many years when a mudslide had sent it into the river.

His father had died in that robbery, shot just outside of town. No way could Stewart ethically be involved in the investigation if finding this evidence opened the case up again. No charges had ever been filed, but everyone had assumed that Lila's father had killed his partner and disappeared with the loot.

He remembered sitting at his desk and staring at the report for a long time, not even being able to zero in on the emotions that were stirred up: anger, confusion, grief. All feelings he'd shut the door on ten years ago to get on with his life.

His mom rose to her feet. "I'm going back to my studio. Call if you need me. There's some soup in the refrigerator you can warm up for Lila if she wants some, and there's always tea."

"Thanks, Mom."

The thing that bothered him the most was that in ten years Lila had not even sent a Christmas card. She was a documentary filmmaker and painter living in Seattle. Anytime he was missing her, he did a Google search on her until the nostalgic feelings subsided and he remembered how deeply she had hurt him.

It wasn't wanting to reconnect or apologize that brought her back to Trident, Montana, but stirring up trouble over the case that had ruined both their lives. Stewart clenched his teeth feeling a rising tension in his chest as Lila came down the hallway. He reined in his emotions. They could talk. He shouldn't jump to conclusions.

Lila was wearing one of his mother's flannel shirts and sweats.

"Did you get warmed up?"

She nodded.

He pointed to a chair opposite him. She sat down and looked at him, waiting for him to speak first. Ten years had been kind to her. She looked even more beautiful. When he'd first met her, he'd been drawn in by her round doe eyes. They'd been assigned to be partners in biology lab.

"You want some soup or tea?"

She shook her head.

Where to begin?

"You could have at least phoned and let me know you were coming." His voice sounded more accusatory than he had intended.

"I did. I left a message on your voice mail."

"On my cell?"

"It was the number that came up when I looked up the Lazy DN Bar ranch."

"The landline." Mostly business calls came in on that line. Someone must have played the message and then forgot to inform him. His mom, younger brother and ranch hand would have checked the messages.

She crossed her arms. "You know why I'm here?"

Her remark was like an electric cattle prod to his back. He jerked to his feet as the intense hurt from ten years ago flooded through him. "That case can't be any of my concern because of my personal link to it. I don't know what you thought you were going to accomplish by showing up in this dramatic way."

She rose to her feet and matched his level in tone of voice. "They aren't releasing information to the press. I want to know what they found in that car…if there are…human remains. You're a sheriff now. You could find out. I have to know what happened to my father. You should care about solving this case."

Stewart felt like a flock of birds were inside his chest. "It's pretty clear what happened. Your father and my father colluded to steal from the safety deposit boxes at the bank where your father worked. Then your father shot mine and disappeared with the loot."

"What about the theory that there was another man involved? I know my father. He was a good man. He was an honest man. Being the bank manager and taking care of this community was important to him. I believe he was coerced into letting your father in to drill those safe-deposit boxes."

"Innocent men don't disappear like that, Lila." He stepped toward her. Seeing the desperation in her eyes made him soften his tone. "You need to just accept that. The case is ten years old. Chances are it won't ever get solved."

"I can't accept it because it's not the truth. You knew what kind of man my father was." Tears welled up in her eyes. She turned away from him.

He moved to rest a hand on her shoulder but thought better of it. She might jerk away from his touch, and he could not take even that small rejection. Just a reminder of how deep a wound she had inflicted when she left town.

"A person came after me on the road to your place, and I was shot at. Doesn't that prove that someone has something to hide?"

"It's bad police work to link what happened to you with finding the getaway car. You need evidence. I didn't hear any shots. Anyway, I sent my deputy out to have a look."

"Why else would someone come after me?"

"Who even knew you were back here?"

"I stopped in town, said hi to a few people and had a burger at the supper club."

So everyone in town would have known once the tongues started wagging. Trident had a population of only eight thousand people.

He doubted his deputy would find much in the rain. But as sheriff, Stewart had to investigate any claim of criminal activity.

"Fine, someone had a road rage moment." She shook her head. "But to shoot at me too? That just doesn't add up. It's too extreme a response."

"Look, I'm not drawing conclusions until I have more information."

A pained look crossed her face, and then she turned her palm upward. "It's bleeding again."

"What did you do?" He was already halfway to the kitchen to grab the first aid kit.

"I fell when I was running."

They weren't exactly shouting at each other, but their tones were clipped and terse.

He opened a drawer, grabbed the first aid kit then returned to the living room. "Give me your hand."

After retrieving disinfectant and gauze, he rested his hand under hers. Their eyes locked momentarily—long enough for him to feel a spark of attraction before she looked away and drew her attention to the floor. Her hand was like silk in his.

"Maybe I shouldn't have come back here." Her words took on a note of sadness.

"A phone call would have sufficed."

"I was afraid you wouldn't take my call. You didn't get the message I left on the ranch phone?"

"My brother or the ranch hand must have taken the message and not told me. Why, I don't know. Sometimes things just get busy."

He'd had ten years to run through scenarios of how he would react if she got in touch with him. Everything from rejecting her to them getting back together.

The calf still lying by the fire let out a cry then struggled to get to its feet. "There's my girl." He looked at Lila. "I've got to take her out to the barn." He moved toward the coatrack to grab his rain gear.

"I'll go with you," she said.

It was clear she wanted to continue to talk. He'd hoped for a reprieve. Her return had sent him into a tailspin. How could a woman have such a hold on him after ten years? Though he had dated some, he clearly had not moved on and had been unable to form a connection with any of the other women he went out with.

Maybe it was less about the love they'd shared and more about the dark crime that blew their worlds apart. He needed time alone to sort through it all. He didn't like thinking about who his father had been. Angry, a bully and known to cheat other ranchers. Stewart had spent the last ten years trying to prove that sometimes the acorn did fall far from the tree.

The steely look in her eyes told him he wouldn't be able to stop her. He tossed a rain poncho toward her. "It's my brother's. It will be a little big on you."

"Thank you."

He pulled his mother's heavy jacket from the hook. "Put this on first."

She slipped the jacket on. He lifted his rain poncho over his head, then picked the calf up and headed toward the door, leaving her to scramble to catch up with him.

He stepped off the porch out into the cold, wet night. He stared up the long driveway. If Lila had been shot at like she said, who had been out there, and why had they wanted to harm her?

TWO

Before she could get the hood of the poncho over her head, rain spattered her face and wet hair. All she wanted from Stewart was a straight answer—that he would help her as much as he could. She couldn't do this alone. And really, after ten years, she felt like the police had given up. Even this new evidence might not spur them to reopen the case.

Though she had found professional success, in many ways, she felt like she would be unable to move on with her life until she knew for sure what had happened to her father. She was an only child, and her mother's mental illness had meant that it was her father she had leaned on. The robbery had taken all the family she'd known.

A month after high school graduation and two weeks after she'd buried her mother, with the wedding invitations all ready to mail out, Lila took the road out of town and just kept driving. After the robbery, her relationship with Stewart cracked. They were just too young and ill-equipped to overcome what may or may not have transpired between their fathers.

Why didn't Stewart care about finding out the truth as much as she did?

She hurried to catch up with Stewart as he stepped into the barn. There was a horse in a stall along with two heifers, one with a newborn of her own.

Stewart approached the other heifer. "Hey, Rosie." He put the calf on the ground. He half-turned, addressing Lila while she stood in the doorway. "This little one's mom rejected her. It happens. Rosie is a good mama who lost her baby. I'm hoping she'll take to this one while she has milk to give."

Lila watched as Stewart nudged the little one toward the heifer. His gentle tone was comforting, like listening to ocean waves. The calf took hesitant steps toward Rosie as the heifer lowered her head and licked its face.

The two animals did a strange dance of stepping forward and back until the calf latched on and nursed. Rosie's tail swung, and she stood still.

The picture of contentment made Lila momentarily forget the angst and grief that had brought her back here. "Success."

Stewart straightened and turned toward her. "Sometimes things work out right." When he smiled like that, she saw something of the Stewart she'd left behind. Not the harsh, hard lines of his features, a man who seemed to be in a permanent state of worry like she'd seen back at the house, but something of the young man she'd fallen in love with.

"Can't you just make a call for me to whoever is in charge of the investigation? The FBI is involved, right?"

"The case went cold." His expression darkened. "I'm sure if there is information they can release to the press, they'll do so eventually."

"Not if they think it would interfere with the investigation. This new evidence means they will reopen the case right?" She stepped toward him. The barn was lit by a single hanging bulb. "All I care about if finding out what happened to my father."

His eyes searched hers. "And then what will you do?"

The problem was if there were remains in the car and they were her father's, it didn't close the case. It opened it wide up. It meant someone else was involved. "I don't know. I want to know for certain what really happened. Don't you?"

Stewart walked over to the stall and petted

the horse who nuzzled him. "Sometimes the easiest answer is the right answer."

It was clear to Lila that Stewart's solution to dealing with the pain of the past was to close the door and move on. Over the years, a thought nagged at her. If they knew for sure that her father hadn't killed his, maybe they never would have broken up.

She drew nearer to him. "I'm sorry I can't let this go. I keep thinking my father is alive and out there somewhere. Maybe my life was threatened if he didn't leave town. Sometimes I'll have a gallery showing or a premier and I feel like he is there on the outskirts of the crowd watching and…being proud of me."

He turned to face her, shaking his head. "You lost more than me, and I am so sorry for that. Let the law handle this. If finding the car brings new evidence to light and opens the case back up, then fine."

"I'm not sure the police care anymore." His remark was a dismissal of her request. His lack of support felt like a slap in the face.

He picked up some straw and tossed it toward where Rosie and the calf were. "Where are you staying?"

"I kept my parents' house and hired a property manager to rent it out for me. It's vacant right now. I already dropped off my suitcase. I thought I'd stay there."

"You'll need a ride back into town. In the morning, we'll look into getting your car pulled out."

She nodded. She knew from the tone of his voice that there would be no more talk about the past.

"I left the keys in the truck. We can go right now. I have to cover the night shift, so just give me a minute to change into my uniform."

Lila waited in the living room while Stewart went upstairs. Music was playing in Cindy's studio. So, she was still working.

Lila stared at the wall of pictures. Most were of Stewart, his brother, Elliot, and his mother. There was only one photograph of Stewart's father, sitting on a horse and looking down in an intimidating way at the photographer.

Stewart came downstairs and she rose to her feet. The uniform accentuated his broad shoulders. She couldn't help but feel drawn to him. The memory of being held by him made her breath catch. Attraction wasn't the basis for a relationship though. "You look nice."

He nodded and grabbed his rain poncho.

They were both silent for most of the ride into town as rain fell at a steady pace. He dropped her off in front of the house she'd grown up in. Dashing to get out of the rain, she hurried up the steps and unlocked the door. She'd taken the time only to place the suitcase inside the foyer. She flicked on a light. The property manager made sure the place was aired out and cleaned when it was vacant, so dust didn't settle on everything. Lila stared out the front window where Stewart sat behind the wheel, letting his truck idle. She waved, and he pulled away from the curb.

She pressed her palm on the glass as rain trickled down. She had to admit that Stewart's reaction to her return had revealed much. Until her conversation with Stewart, she hadn't attached words to the fragile hope that had brought her back here. If they could get answers about what really happened ten years ago, maybe she and Stewart could mend the chasm between them. She now knew the answer to that question was no. Some things were just too broken to fix, and Stewart didn't want to open the Pandora's box of the past.

She switched on a light and stared at her childhood home that didn't look anything like her childhood home. She'd given the property manager carte blanche to decorate in a way that would make it an attractive vacation rental. Lila wandered down the hall to her old room. She removed pillows from the bed and pulled back the covers. She was too exhausted to change into pajamas.

Closing her eyes, she waited for sleep to overtake her. Hours later, she woke in total darkness to faint sounds? Her heart squeezed tight. Someone moving around in the house? She held her breath. Then sat up. Her pulse drummed in her ears as she listened. Soft footsteps. She hadn't imagined an intruder, and it hadn't been part of a dream.

Someone was in the house.

Her heartbeat kicked up a notch.

A soft, thudding noise reached her ears. A person moving through the house almost noiselessly. The footsteps got louder. He or she was coming down the hall toward her room. She burst out of the bed and raced toward the door, seeking to close it and lock it.

A heavy weight was on the other side as she pushed. A man groaned. Lila slammed her whole body against the door. It was no use. The door flung open. She dashed through the open door. A hand reached out for her, pulled her back by grabbing her shirttail. Beating the air with her fists, she swung around hoping to hit something. She made contact several times. When he let go of her, she ran down the dark hallway.

Where was her phone? Had she left her purse in the rental car or brought it with her?

The house was pitch-black. She'd not left on any lights. She stumbled around in the dark and fell over something. Her hand caught the soft arm of the sofa before she went down.

Three pounding footsteps and then pressure on the back of her neck. Her near fall had given away her location. Twisting her body, she tried to escape his grasp. She turned and pinched flesh.

He let out a yelp.

She held her arms out in front of her and moved across the floor. Her bare feet made almost no noise. Finally finding a wall, she pressed against it. His footsteps came one at a time with long pauses between.

She was afraid her heavy breathing would give her away in the darkness.

Why didn't he turn on a light to find her? He didn't want her to see who he was. That had to be it.

The footsteps came closer as she tried to remember the arrangement of the furniture. She wasn't even sure where she was at in the living room.

He was close now. Maybe five feet from her. Her hand reached out and touched a floor lamp. She grabbed the base, rose to her feet and started swinging. She hit her target several times.

Then the room fell silent. Gasping for breath, she held on to the lamp. Then she saw the blinking light of her phone. She had put it on the entryway table. Dropping the lamp, she raced across the floor and grabbed it. The screen lit up.

A body slammed into hers before she could shine a light on her assailant. She dropped her phone.

A hand pressed on her neck. He was so close she could hear him gasp for air. She reached out, clawing at the air hoping to scratch him. The pressure on her neck subsided.

She could see her phone three feet away on the floor. She crawled toward it as the man grabbed her by the ankle. Her fingers wrapped around the phone as she pulled free. The glow of the phone showed her where the powder room was. She got to her feet and ran toward it, slamming the door shut and locking it. The assailant banged on the door three times. She flicked on the light and pressed 911 on the phone.

"What is your emergency?"

"Someone is in my house."

"Are you in a safe place?"

"I'm locked in the bathroom. He's on the other side of the door."

Then she heard retreating footsteps and a door slamming.

Lila collapsed on the bathroom floor.

The call came in at 3:00 a.m. Stewart recognized the address right away. He jumped in the sheriff's car and headed across town. Lila's house was dark when he arrived. He knocked on the door and waited. The front door was locked. He circled the house and found an unlatched window.

He opened it and yelled. "Lila." Fully aware that the culprit might still be on the premises, his hand hovered over his gun. He didn't see or hear anything on the outside of the house. He couldn't take a chance that Lila was inside being hurt. Returning to the front door, he slammed his body against it, flinging it open. "Lila, it's me."

As he walked through the house, he feared that something had happened to her. He increased his pace, flipping on lights as he went searching each corner for the intruder. His free hand hovered over his gun. All the interior doors were open but one. Light spilled out from beneath the powder room door. He tried the knob. Locked. He tapped lightly.

"Lila, are you in there?"

He heard footsteps and then the door flew open. She fell into his arms.

"Someone was here. He came after me." Her voice was filled with anguish as he held her.

Though he needed the details of the break-in, now was not the time to ask sheriff questions. "It's all right. I'm here." He held her until she calmed down and stepped away from his embrace.

"Did you see the guy?"

She shook her head. "He kept the lights off on purpose."

"Come with me through the house. Tell me if anything was disturbed or is missing."

"I really didn't take in the layout of the house or what was here. I just went right to bed." She met his gaze. "I don't think he was here to steal anything."

He led her down the hallway. "It's good to look anyway." Once in the living room, she surveyed the space.

A floor lamp lay on its side.

"My suitcase is knocked over," she said. "I don't know about anything else. I didn't take note of how things were arranged."

"There was an unlatched window. He must have gotten in that way."

Lila sat down on the sofa. Her face had

drained of color, and her gestures were jerky as she touched her palm to her chest.

She was clearly not in any condition to talk about what had happened. "I have to file a report. If you remember more details, let me know."

Looking up at him, her gaze was focused and piercing. "This place has been unoccupied for a week. If he was here to rob the house, he could have done it at any time. He came here because I was here. He came after me."

"Are you saying someone was watching the house?"

"He must have been." She stood up, shaking her head. "I could hear him moving through the house. He was trying to find which bedroom I was in. He pushed on the door I was trying to shut."

That was speculation on Lila's part. How could she tell from hearing footsteps what the intruder was doing? Maybe he had come to rob the place and had not expected it to be occupied. "Look, you probably don't feel safe staying here tonight. I'll take you back to my place until we can figure something out."

"You don't believe me? This is connected to the getaway car being found. Someone doesn't want me in Trident."

Stewart hated that he could not separate his

mixed emotions toward Lila from doing his job as a police officer. He tried to keep his response professional. "It could be connected."

She shook her head. "You want this case to go away. Your life, your mother's life got better when your dad died. Your only job was to prove that you weren't like your father. That's probably why you ran for sheriff."

The comment hit too close to home. He'd had a lot of fences to mend after his dad's death. His father not being in the picture had given him, his mother and brother a second chance. "I can't get into this. Grab your stuff. I'll take you back to my place until we can figure out other arrangements. I still have a shift to finish."

The wounded look on her face told him that his words had come out more forcefully than he'd intended. Lifting her chin, she rose to her feet and padded across the floor and slipped into the shoes she'd left by the suitcase. She didn't even make eye contact with him.

"This isn't my case, Lila. Bank robbery is a federal crime. If it is reopened, the FBI will be in charge. I will focus on who broke into your house and why. I don't know if it connects to the robbery."

She pulled the handle of her suitcase up abruptly. "I'm ready to go."

He knew that lilt in her voice meant there would be no more discussion, and no amount of him explaining how the law worked would change her mind. Lila Rose Christie could be incredibly stubborn.

She turned out the lights before stepping outside. When he'd banged down the door he'd damaged the lock. "I'll see to it that this is fixed tonight."

Lila thanked him.

Once they were in the sheriff's car, Stewart sent a text to his mom. "My mom might still be awake working on some project. She keeps kind of strange hours since she became a full-time artist."

"What about your brother and the ranch hand?"

"Elliot lives in town with his wife Missy and kid. He has a second job. The ranch hand Roy does his own thing. He has separate living quarters."

"I remember Roy. He's been with the ranch for a long time."

"Fifteen years. He was a great help after Dad died. He can't physically do what he used to, but I feel like I owe him a job for his loyalty and putting up with my dad all those years."

Stewart drove past the dark windows of

Main Street and out to the city limits. At least the rain had stopped. When they arrived at the house, there was a single light on. His mom's studio.

He checked his phone. His mom had responded that she would get Lila settled in for the night. "Mom is expecting you. Just knock on the studio door."

Stewart got out and helped Lila with her suitcase. He climbed back into the sheriff's SUV and watched as she made her way up the stairs and stepped inside. She had narrowly avoided harm three times now if what she said was true. He couldn't help but think that if she would just leave town and wait for news about what had been found in that car, the trouble she had stirred up would go away. He was going to suggest that to her in the morning.

He stared out into the darkness and then tapped his fist on the steering wheel. Who was he kidding? Maybe the reason he wanted her to leave was because all the unresolved feelings about her rose to the surface, the hurt and the love. If she went away, maybe he could get those emotions back in the box he kept them in.

As he turned around and headed back toward town, he hoped that Lila would be safe at the ranch house.

THREE

Lila stepped inside the dark house. Leaving her suitcase at the door, she headed down the hallway to the room where the light was on. The studio door was open, and classical music spilled out from a speaker while Stewart's mother worked attaching clay to a sculpture of a horse.

The older woman glanced up when Lila stepped inside. Lila couldn't quite read that look on Mrs. Duncan's face. As a teacher, Cindy had been kind and encouraging to her students, a positivity powerhouse while she was living a nightmare of abuse at home.

Though she attempted to cover it with a wooden smile, the expression on the older woman's face suggested discomfort. Maybe she shared the same feelings as her son about Lila's return. Lila's intent hadn't been to open old wounds, but to find answers so she could move on with her own life.

Mrs. Duncan stepped away from the sculpture. "Let me wash my hands, and I'll get you set up in a bedroom."

Lila stepped into the studio. "That's really beautiful work, Mrs. Duncan."

The older woman stepped over to a sink and turned on the water. "You can call me Cindy. I'm not your teacher anymore and thank you for the compliment."

"Thank you for putting me up for the night. This whole thing has not gone like I'd hoped."

Cindy grabbed a towel and dried her hands. "What did you expect?" The question held a tone of accusation.

"I guess I thought that Stewart would be more supportive of finding some resolve to this case," said Lila.

"I think that he's moved on, Lila."

"As long as it remains unsolved, this whole town thinks of my father as a murderer and a thief."

Cindy tossed the towel on the counter and walked toward Lila. "I mourned the loss of my husband when he died. He was an angry, abusive man, but that didn't mean I didn't try to love him. I have built a life without him, and Stewart was able to become something more than the son of the meanest man in the county." The harsh edge left her voice. "It's been ten years, Lila. Sometimes we never get the answers we want."

It was clear that she was alone in her fight for the truth of what really happened. Lila nodded. "I'm sorry, but I can't let this go."

"I'll show you to the guest room." Cindy led her through the living room and up a staircase, stopping to grab fresh towels out of the linen closet.

When she looked in, the guest room with its queen sized bed and quilt, paintings of flowers on the wall gave off a cozy feel. "Beautiful décor."

"Just country simple. Nothing fancy. Breakfast is at eight." After Lila stepped inside, Cindy closed the bedroom door and left.

For the second time Lila climbed under the covers fully dressed. She knew what she would do in the morning once her car was pulled out of the mud. She was going to drive to the site where the getaway car had been found. If she had to do this alone, she would.

Lila awoke hours later surprised at how well she'd slept. She showered and changed and went downstairs. Through the large living room windows, she saw that her rental car was parked outside. Stewart must have taken care of that while she'd slept.

She heard laughter from the kitchen. The

aroma of coffee and bacon reached her nose even before she entered the room. Stewart's younger brother, Elliot, sat at the table with the ranch hand. Roy's face was leathery from having spent so much time outside. He had been the Senior Mr. Duncan's drinking buddy before his death. Both men watched Lila with a wary eye. Lila nodded at them, not sure if they had been told she was staying here. They hadn't seemed surprised to see her.

Cindy smiled. "There's coffee and pancakes and bacon, if you'd like."

"I'll just have some coffee. I won't be here long. I have a drive ahead of me. I'm going to go to Lewis County."

Cindy set her coffee cup on the counter. "Where they found the getaway car?"

A tension settled into the room. The two men exchanged glances. Roy shot up from his chair. "I'm mending fence in the north field. Gonna take most of the day." He stomped out of the room and through the back door.

"Where is Stewart?"

"He's sleeping. His shift ended three hours ago. I think you should talk to him before you go anywhere," said Cindy.

"Why? He's already made it clear he doesn't want to help me."

Elliot pushed his chair back. "I'm going

into town for some supplies. Good to see you again, Lila."

The last time she'd seen Elliot, he was a gangly twelve-year-old, and now he was married and had a kid.

"You too, Elliot," said Lila.

He stood up and made his way to the living room and then stepped outside.

Lila turned to face Cindy. "Stewart has made it clear I'm on my own where getting information about the getaway car is concerned. He doesn't want to help me. Not in his capacity as sheriff and not for old time's sake. Fine with me, but he doesn't get to dictate what I choose to do."

Cindy stepped toward her looking her in the eye. "Please understand how hard this is for him. He fell apart after you left."

Lila didn't know if that was true or not. Stewart had not said as much. Yet, neither of them had moved on to other relationships. "How could I be married to someone who believed my father had killed his father?"

"It's not that I expected the two of you would rush into each other's arms. It's just when I heard your voice on the phone last night, I thought you had come back to heal some wounds."

Hadn't she hoped that too? "That getaway

car was the first glimmer of hope I had felt in ten years that I would finally get answers that made sense. I've hired detectives who couldn't get any traction. The investigators gave up." Lila headed for the door. "I'll be out of your hair in ten minutes. I've just got to grab my suitcase."

Cindy reached for her arm. "I'd heard that Richard had mounting medical bills trying to get your mother the help she needed."

"That was just gossip." Her father had been a caretaker by nature, wanting to protect Lila. Once her father was declared legally dead. She had access to his financials that did reveal some debt. But she knew her father's character. He wouldn't steal to get money. "Again, thank you for your hospitality." She didn't like the way Cindy had implied her father would have a motive for the robbery.

Lila left the room feeling like she'd been run through a paper shredder. She grabbed the suitcase, loaded it into the rental car and sat behind the wheel. She gave the house one last look. If she and Stewart had gotten married like they'd planned, she'd probably be living in this house. They would have had three or four children by now.

She started the car, switched into Reverse

and cranked the wheel to get turned around. The car made a low-grade screeching sound. "What on earth?"

When she looked up, a sleepy-eyed barefoot Stewart stood on the porch. He hurried down the stairs, indicating that she needed to roll down her window.

"The tow truck driver thought the axle might be damaged."

"So I can't drive it?"

"I wouldn't. You can take it up with the rental car company. Maybe they can get you a replacement."

Lila pressed her lips together and gripped the wheel. Liquid warmed the corners of her eyes. So much for a grand exit.

Don't cry in front of him.

He straightened up so she had full view of his hips and chest. He was dressed in sweats and a ratty T-shirt that had seen better days. "Where were you going in such an all-fired hurry, anyway?"

She pushed open the door which forced him to take a step back. Now she could look him in the eyes. "I was going to drive out to the place where the car was found."

"I'm sure it's a sealed-off crime scene."

She shut the door then stepped away from the car. "You could find out when they open it back up to the public. That might be the last place my father was before he disappeared… or died." This time she couldn't stop the tears.

He wrapped an arm around her. "Why don't you come back inside and make some calls to get another car?"

She saw so much compassion in his face. "I'm sorry I woke you."

"You didn't wake me. My mom did." He escorted her up the steps. "It's all right. I've got some calls to make myself."

She felt bad for Stewart operating on only a couple of hours of sleep. It made his kindness all that more touching. He was the opposite of his father in that way, not prone to anger and infinitely patient.

She stepped back into the house, which was quiet. Through the kitchen window, she saw that Cindy had stepped outside and was walking toward the chicken house. She could hear Stewart in a room down the hall talking to someone. Lila retrieved her phone and called the car rental company and explained the situation. They agreed to give her a different rental and to arrange for the defunct car to be towed.

Stewart emerged from wherever he had been talking on the phone. He walked over to the kitchen counter and poured himself a cup of coffee. After plating up cold pancakes and bacon, he put them in the microwave. “Did you get things set up?”

She nodded. “I’ll need a ride to the rental car place.”

“I can do that.” He pulled a piece of paper out of his pocket and handed it to her.

She read the man’s name and the phone number and looked at him with a questioning expression.

“That’s the agent who was in charge of the investigation years ago. There are some things he just can’t tell you.”

“I understand.” She typed the number and name into her phone. Stewart’s gesture meant a great deal to her.

“There were no human remains in the car. A lot of the evidence was destroyed because it was underwater so long. It will probably just be another dead end.”

She rose to her feet. “That means my father might still be alive.”

Stewart’s voice intensified. “What if you do find him, Lila, and it turns out he is a murderer and a thief, and he’s been on the run this whole time? How does that make your life better?”

“It would at least give me an answer.”

Stewart stared out the window. “I’ll take

you to go get the rental car and then maybe you should think about going back to Seattle."

It was clear he just wanted her and the trouble she seemed to have brought with her gone. "All my parents' personal stuff is in the garage at the old house. I just had the property manager put it in storage. I'm here now. I think I'm ready to sort through it."

He studied her for a long moment. "If that's what you want to do."

"Did your deputy find anything last night?"

"Just your car stuck in the mud."

"I imagine the shell casings got lost in the mud too. The back bumper must show that someone hit me from behind."

"Lila, it's not that I don't believe you. It's just that there is nothing to work with here. How would I even track the guy down? I'm trying to do my job."

A hundred emotions collided within her. "Don't the attacks on me prove that someone didn't want me here?"

"Not necessarily. You need evidence that links the crimes. You can't even describe the guy or the vehicle that ran you off the road."

It seemed that Stewart had chosen to deal with all this acting in his role as sheriff, not as someone who had a personal stake in finding out the truth. "I'm just saying that it is a stunning coincidence to have this happen when I get back to town."

He let out a heavy breath. "Where is the rental car place at?"

Some things about a man didn't change. When Stewart didn't want to talk about something, he changed the subject. "By the airport. Sorry it's a bit of a drive."

"If you don't mind, we'll take the scenic route. I'm leasing some land over in that area. I have to check on the cattle I put out to pasture."

Within minutes they were in Stewart's truck headed up the road and out into the country. Stewart took the truck up a knobby ridge and stopped. He grabbed some binoculars from the crew-cab seat and then set the hand brake. "This might take a few minutes. I have to do a head count. You can come with me or stay in the truck. It's up to you."

"I'll go with you," she said.

They got out of the truck. Lila had a view of a long, steep draw and a few black dots at the bottom that had to be cows. The wind picked up as they made their way downhill. The breeze and the sun on her face felt nice. Hadn't they done something similar a hundred times when they were dating? She'd enjoyed helping him with the ranch chores.

Stewart drew the binoculars up to his face. He seemed to be focused on an area beyond a cluster of trees.

Though it was hard to tell with the wind, she thought she heard noise behind her by the truck. They had hiked far enough down that only the front part of the vehicle was visible.

She turned her attention back to where Stewart was looking, still not seeing anything that might be a cow. A rumbling screech above her caused her to look back up at the ridge.

Lila screamed as the truck rolled down the slope straight toward them.

It took less than a second for Stewart to comprehend what was happening. He lifted Lila up and out of the way of the truck's trajectory. They landed in the tall grass as he heard the crush of metal. The truck flipped twice before landing upside down. His heart sank. His beautiful truck looked like a crushed soda can.

How on earth had that happened? He'd parked in a flat area and set the hand brake. After all that had happened, he suspected sabotage.

He rolled away from Lila. "Are you okay?"

She nodded and sat up.

He still couldn't process that his truck had been totaled. "We'll have to hike down to the wreck. Hopefully our phones survived."

"I left my purse in there."

Already they were encountering bits of debris that had been thrown out of the cab and bed of the truck: blankets he used to warm calves, a bag of feed, a gas can and tools.

Once at the truck, it was obvious he wasn't going to find his phone. He'd left it on the dashboard. It must have fallen out in the crash, and it was probably broken into a hundred pieces.

Lila gazed up and down the hill. "We have a better chance of spotting my purse. The phone would have been protected. It should still work." She hiked back up the hill moving in a serpentine pattern while she stared at the ground.

He searched as well, picking up a wrench that he found. His gaze went to where the truck had been parked. He felt a tightening in his chest right before he heard the zing of a rifle shot. He ran toward Lila and gathered her in his arms.

The shot had come from somewhere above them. He guided her toward the truck just as another shot was fired.

"Get behind the truck. It'll give us some cover."

He pressed his back against the upside-down bed. When he lifted his head and peered around a tire, he couldn't see anyone. Another shot whizzed past his head. He hunkered down beside Lila.

"We can't get out by hiking back up. There's no place to take cover, and he's still up there." Stewart pointed to where he thought the shots had come from.

She rested her face in her hands. "Then what are we going to do? Wait him out?"

Stewart looked downhill where the cattle grazed. This was not his land. It was a leased field. He wasn't familiar with the area. He didn't know what was beyond those trees. Now that he'd seen an attack firsthand, he was forced to admit that Lila was right. Her return had made someone very nervous. Had there been a third man involved in the robbery, and had he been living in this town the whole time? Or had he too returned when the new evidence had surfaced?

"I say we head down this draw and through those trees. Maybe there's someone living there. We can call for help."

She craned her neck. "What if he follows us?"

That was a possibility. "Crawl straight out from the truck. He won't be able to see us for quite a while. Not until the land flattens out. And then make a run for those trees."

She nodded.

They moved slowly, both of them glancing over their shoulders. Stewart thought he saw a man hunkered down in the tall grass. Once the land flattened, they rose and sprinted toward the trees just as another shot was fired.

FOUR

Lila gasped for air as her feet pounded the grassy earth. Another shot echoed around her. She half expected to fall to the ground from the impact of the bullet, but it had missed her. While she focused on the trees up ahead, she willed herself to keep going despite the paralyzing fear.

When he got too far ahead of her, Stewart slowed his pace, so they were running side by side. He ushered her toward the copse of aspens which were just budding out.

Both of them slowed but kept moving. When she looked over her shoulder, the trees blocked her view.

Would the man with the rifle pursue them down into the valley, or would he give up?

Several cows and calves grazed close to the trees. They lifted their heads and stared blankly while still chewing their cud as Lila and Stewart jogged past.

The trees thinned out, and they encountered even more cows. Even though they slowed to a walk, her heart was still pounding from the rush of adrenaline. Several minutes had passed without any more shots being fired.

This act of violence had to be connected to the other three assaults. Though she didn't want to believe someone would be so relentless. Stewart was all about solid police work. She didn't want to jump to conclusions. The man with the rifle had taken a shot at Stewart as well. "I don't suppose you have had some dispute with another rancher around here?"

"None that I am aware of. It was pretty competitive to get the lease on this land." Stewart studied the flat terrain in front of him. "I just can't imagine someone being so upset that they would decide to shoot at me."

Once they walked beyond the cluster of trees, the flat grassy land was dotted with more cows. "Maybe something you did in relationship to your work as sheriff?"

He shook his head. "I don't know. Could be. People don't like being thrown in jail."

She could not bring herself to ask the question about the most obvious reason they were under assault.

He turned to face her. "I see that you are

being cautious because of what I said earlier about evidence. You were right. Your return has stirred something up."

"Thank you." She wished that his words brought a sense of victory. But their situation was too dire to even feel triumphant about his change of heart.

There were no buildings or even a fence to indicate that they were any place close to people. "How far are we going to walk?"

Stewart edged closer to her. Touching her arm in a protective way as he glanced over his shoulder.

She turned to scan the landscape. Though they had not seen the shooter running toward them, there were clusters of tall grass where a man could hide.

"Let's move parallel to the road then arc up and away from the crash site. We're more likely to run into help on the road."

More likely to run into the shooter too. It did not appear that he had followed them down into the valley. They could walk for hours this way and not run into anyone. Stewart's plan was the best choice when there were no good options.

The sky began to darken, threatening rain as they made their way along the valley floor. Having caught their breath, they started to jog through tall grass, moving for what was maybe half a mile before Stewart worked his way upward at a diagonal. They had gone less than a mile by her estimate. If the shooter hadn't followed them down, what if he were waiting for them to emerge by patrolling the road?

The trek grew steep, slowing them down.

As they drew closer to the road, the rain came down and intensified. The path to get up to the road was at an extreme angle. Lila had to step sideways to make any progress. When a vehicle rumbled by, Stewart crouched and then walked parallel to the road again. Did he think that might be the shooter?

As she listened to the sound of the engine fade, she realized the truck had been going so fast, there would have been no way for them to get up to the road in time to be seen if it had been someone who could offer aid.

She prayed they would encounter another car and that it wouldn't be the man with the rifle.

When they finally stepped onto the road, the rain had soaked through her clothes. The sight of nothing but rolling countryside for miles filled her with despair.

"Sorry about this." He edged a little closer to her. "We have no choice but to keep going."

"I don't remember even seeing a farmhouse once we turned onto the dirt road that led this way." Trembling, she crossed her arms over her body.

She looked behind her at the empty road which was quickly becoming muddy. At least she didn't see any headlights coming toward them from where they'd been shot at.

The rain kept falling. Both of them were shivering and cold by the time they took shelter by some trees not too far from the road. The dark sky indicated that the storm was not going to let up anytime soon.

For two people who had once loved each other, it seemed like they would have more to talk about. Every subject though had the potential for conflict.

She listened to the symphonic patter of the rain, trying to ignore the silent tension between them.

"I should have just taken you directly to get your rental car. You wouldn't be here in the middle of this mess."

She chose her words carefully knowing that every topic of conversation seemed to cause them to butt heads. "This may not have happened to you if I had already been dropped off."

"He shot at both of us," said Stewart. "I'm

just sorry, is all. I'm sorry that you came back here and everything has gone so wrong."

"I don't regret it," she said. "I will follow any lead to figure out what happened to my father."

Stewart uttered a single syllable as if he was going to respond. Instead, he just shook his head. If the time they had been together since she'd returned to Trident had proven anything, it was that all conversations seemed to lead to land mines. She appreciated that he had exercised such self-control.

"We can't stay under this tree forever. Let's just focus on getting out of here. Rain is going to wash away any evidence of who the shooter was, but I've still got to file a report and get someone out here."

It was clear that Stewart felt most comfortable putting on his sheriff's hat and keeping his mind on his job. They trudged back out to the road. She walked with her head down and her arms crossed over her chest, grateful that the rain hid her tears.

She barely heard the rumble of an engine over the sound of the rain and the intensity of her thoughts. Stewart tugged her shirtsleeve and guided her off the road. The truck was coming from the direction where they had been shot at.

When she stared down the road, she could

not make out the model of the truck at this distance. She only hoped it wasn't the shooter coming back to finish them off.

Stewart placed a protective arm around Lila's back as they stepped away from the middle of the road. He was prepared to either wave the truck down or run for cover. He had not seen the vehicle that the shooter had arrived in.

Lila's shivering and slumped posture cut him to the core. Regardless of how he felt about her return, his instinct was always to protect her. To see her so cold and distraught upset him.

The truck slowed as it drew closer. Once he saw that the model was from the 1950s and the truck bed was filled with something covered by a tarp, he relaxed. The truck was distinctive, and he knew who it belonged to: Dale, the junkman.

The truck rolled to a stop, and the window came down. Dale stuck his head out as rain pattered on his leathery face. White hair stuck out from beneath his worn baseball hat.

"Sheriff Duncan, what are you doing out here in the freezing cold with this pretty lady?"

"It's a long story, Dale. I don't suppose you could give us a lift."

"I'm just headed up the road a piece to drop some stuff off at home. You can call for someone to come get you from there. Get yourself dried off while you wait."

"Sounds good," said Stewart. "Thank you."

Lila had lifted her head when Dale rolled down the window. Stewart ushered her toward the passenger side of the truck and opened the door for her so she could get in first.

He climbed in behind her, grateful for the blast of the warm air as he closed the door.

After shifting and rolling forward, Dale spoke to Lila. "I don't believe we've met."

"I'm Lila Rose Christie. I used to live here."

"Oh, yeah." Dale was silent for a moment before squinting and leaning forward to peer through the windshield. "I know the rain is good for the land, but this feels like overkill to me. Turn the whole place into a mud bog."

No doubt Dale had heard the gossip about her return. Stewart was glad that he chose not to pry and instead talk about a safe topic like the weather.

"Yes, it's starting to feel like Montana has a monsoon season," said Stewart.

Within ten minutes, Dale's expansive junkyard came into view. In addition to the old cars and appliances surrounded by a fence, there was a trailer and a metal warehouse with two garage-sized doors. Dale turned off onto the dirt road that led to his property. He parked in front of the mobile home.

"Go on inside. You can use the landline. I lost my cell phone the other day," said Dale. "I'm going to take the truck into the shop so I don't have to unload in the rain."

"I can give you a hand with that if you like," said Stewart.

"I appreciate that, but why don't the two of you go inside and get warmed up first? I'll be in shortly."

As the rain continued to fall, Stewart got out and waited for Lila. They ran the few feet to the trailer and up four steps. The door was unlocked.

Heat from a woodstove engulfed Stewart as they stepped inside. A golden retriever with gray on her muzzle rested on a bed by the stove.

"Hey, Belle," said Stewart.

The dog thumped her tail but did not get up.

"Didn't Dale have an old retriever named Belle ten years ago? I seem to remember seeing her ride around in his truck."

"This is a different dog. He just gets a new golden when the other one passes and names her Belle."

Lila pulled a chair up by the stove while

Stewart looked for the phone. Water dripped off his hair. He found the phone under a newspaper and called his brother, who said he'd be out there to get them soon.

Lila held her hands out toward the stove. "I suppose he has some towels around here that we can use to dry off with, but I don't want to be nosy."

Stewart came and stood by the stove. Just being in the warm truck and now close to the stove had helped stave off the impending hyperthermia.

Dale came back in the house and retrieved some towels for them before going back outside. Stewart patted his clothes somewhat dry and stopped the water from dripping from his hair.

As he stood warming himself, it finally sunk in that he had lost his beloved truck. That was the least of his worries though. To jump to the conclusion that the attempt on his and Lila's life was related to the cold case involving their fathers would be bad police work.

He was inclined to believe her though. This last assault had made it clear that someone was out to get Lila and didn't mind taking him out as collateral. Or was he also a target?

FIVE

Lila rushed to the trailer window when she heard the rumble of a truck outside. Stewart's brother, Elliot, was here. While Stewart had gone outside to help Dale unload in the shop, she was grateful for the reprieve from the tense silence that settled between her and Stewart anytime they were alone.

She waved at Elliot from inside, and he waved back but then pointed toward the shop. Though she didn't have a view of the shop from this angle, she assumed that either Dale or Stewart had called Elliot over to help finish with the unloading.

Rain trailed down the window, and she returned to the warm place by the fire. Belle rose from her bed and stood beside her, looking up at her with big brown eyes. "Do you need some petting?"

The dog wagged her tail.

Though her clothes were still damp, she was no longer cold.

The door burst open, and Stewart poked his head in. "Ready to go?"

A few minutes later, Lila found herself sandwiched between the two brothers in the cab of the truck.

Stewart explained in detail about the lost truck and being shot at.

Elliot whistled. "Pretty serious stuff, huh? What do you think is going on?"

Stewart glanced at Lila. "We're trying to figure that out."

Elliot had been a boy when the bank robbery had happened. She wasn't sure how much Stewart had shared with him since her return.

The brothers exchanged small talk about ranch business. Seattle was only a long day's drive from Trident, yet she was struck by how different her world had become from talk of changing up the feed for the pregnant cows and fence repair. Her work as a filmmaker took her all over the world. Stewart lived a settled small-town life with people like Dale that he'd known for years.

She met and worked with all kinds of interesting people, but her ties to them were very loose. She was close to two women who attended her Bible study. She stared out the window at the fields just starting to turn green.

Much as she admired Stewart's connection to his community, if the last two days had proven anything, it was that she didn't belong here anymore.

Elliot shifted in his seat. "One of our neighbors up the hill said he thought he saw lights by the old homestead. Cows sometimes wander over to that area."

"I'll go have a look when the rain let's up." Stewart turned slightly to address Lila. "Some of the other ranchers have reported missing cows. We're not sure, but we think we might be dealing with cattle rustlers."

Lila nodded. Lost cows for whatever reason were lost income, so something like that was fairly serious.

"It just seems like we would have found one or two of the dead cows if they were just wandering off and getting trapped somewhere," said Elliot.

Stewart stared out the window. "I've got some sheriff business to take care of with my truck and being shot at. Then I need to figure out what I'm going to do for a work truck."

"You can borrow mine if I don't need it for farm stuff. Missy has her car. I'm sure Mom will let you use her car to go into town until the insurance settles up."

"I can't take Mom's car into work. That would leave her stranded." Stewart shook his head. "I'll figure something out."

Because she hadn't been able to get her rental car yet, Lila was no more mobile than he was.

The ranch house came into view, and anxiety twisted through her. She'd vowed not to leave Trident until she had some answers about what had happened to her father. Being stranded at the Lazy DN Bar was not what she'd anticipated. Dealing with how uncomfortable Cindy seemed to be when she was around felt like more than Lila could handle. Once she got her rental car, she'd stay somewhere else. Maybe she could talk Stewart into letting his deputy provide some protection.

Elliot parked his truck close to the porch. "I've got some cows to check on in the north field. I'll be back as soon as I can."

Lila noticed that the defunct rental car had been towed away.

As Elliot drove away, they rushed toward the porch and the rain pelted them. Stewart's arm had gone across her back, and he pulled her close. When they got to the shelter of the porch, he stepped away awkwardly.

His intent had probably simply been to shield her from the rain. The gesture was one that he would have done ten years ago without thinking. Old habits die hard.

She stepped away as well.

He pushed open the door.

Music spilling down the hallway indicated that Mrs. Duncan was in her studio.

Stewart placed his wet hat on the coatrack. “I’m going to change into dry clothes and deal with as much of the work as I can on the phone. I can get my deputy to come get me for my shift tonight. I know you’re still without a car. We both will need new phones. I’ll ask him to grab some in town.”

“Maybe your mom can take me to get my rental car?”

“That would be great if she could. I have a lot to do. When the music stops, she’s no longer in deep-artist mode, so that’s the best time to catch her.”

His suggestion felt like a brush-off. Why was she being so sensitive after she was trying to come up with a plan to get protection from his deputy? The yo-yo emotions were a bit much to take. “I’ll try to ask her when she’s no longer working.”

Stewart stepped closer to her. “Given what

has happened, please have Mom follow you back into town and don't go anywhere alone."

The caution made sense, but she hated the way it made her feel like a prisoner and dependent on him. "Maybe your deputy could provide some protection when I went into town to deal with the house."

Stewart pressed his lips together. A response that she knew meant he wasn't totally for the idea. "We'll work something out."

He disappeared down the hall opposite from where his mother's studio was. Lila trudged upstairs. After a hot shower and changing into dry clothes, she lay down just to close her eyes for a minute but ended up falling into a deep sleep. Her growling stomach woke her. When she lifted her head off the pillow and gazed out the window, the sky indicated that it was late afternoon.

Her bedroom faced the side of the house with a view of the barn and several heavily pregnant cows in one corral. The other corral contained three horses. One she recognized from ten years ago. Houdini had been so named because he liked to escape the pens he was confined in. Stewart had bought him as a colt.

She lay in bed listening to the sound of voices downstairs, and then a door slammed and a vehicle started up. By the time she headed downstairs, the house had fallen silent. Even Cindy's music was not playing.

Once in the living room, the only noise she heard was coming from the kitchen. The soft padding of footsteps. Stewart stood staring out the window, sipping from a mug. He turned when she entered the room.

"Hey, you must have crashed, huh?"

"The day took a lot out of me."

"You want some coffee?"

She shook her head. "Where is everyone?"

"Mom ran into town to see a friend. Roy and Elliot had some business to take care of in Trident as well. Little brother left his truck. I was going to check out the old homestead before I headed out to work. Why don't you come with me?"

He probably didn't want her to be alone in the house. "Sure. Do you have something quick to eat? I haven't had anything all day."

He opened the refrigerator. "I can heat you up a burrito if you don't mind taking it with us. I need to be back in time for my deputy to pick me up."

A few minutes later, they were both sitting in the cab of Elliot's truck. The rain had stopped, but the road was still slick with mud. She took a bite of the burrito.

It was a ten-minute drive on the rutty road to get to the ruins of the original house that had been built when Stewart's great-great-grandfather had homesteaded the land. "Did you find out any more about the person who shot at us?"

"Deputy Swain found a partial tire track that he took a mold of just in case it's significant."

The homestead came into view. There was a building that had been a barn now leaning at a slant. The logs were weathered and gray. Only the foundation remained of the house. Trees and bushes almost obscured it from view. When they had first started dating in high school, he had taken her out here, proudly explaining the family history.

He parked the truck. They both got out. Several cows grazed not too far from the dilapidated structures.

She hurried to match his stride. "What are you even looking for?"

Stewart stopped and stared out at the grazing cattle. "If our neighbor said he saw lights down here, maybe it was someone scouting the place to see if it was accessible to a truck and trailer to load a cow or two and take off with them. I'm just looking for evidence that someone was here recently."

Stewart walked up the road, probably looking for tire tracks. Her attention was drawn toward the old homestead as the memories whirled through her head. When she came out to the ranch and they wanted to be alone, Stewart would take her out here. He had kissed her for the first time here. She stopped only a few feet from the foundation, wondering if the place was bringing back memories for Stewart as well.

He was some distance from her up the road half turned away and focused on the ground. Maybe he had simply put all those memories in a mental closet and locked the door just like he'd done with what had happened to their fathers.

She noticed several empty pop cans and iced tea bottles around the homestead that could have been here for years. On the other side of the foundation was a tangle of brush and undergrowth. There was something on the ground off to the side of the foundation. Something shiny caught her eye. She leaned over and picked up a silver button.

Stewart walked toward her. "There's no reason why the thieves would be rooting around this area if they were scouting the best escape route."

"I know. I was just thinking about the times

you and I came out here." She looked into his brown eyes.

Color rose up in Stewart's cheeks. She took a step toward him, her eyes searching his.

He shook his head but said nothing. So he did remember, but he didn't want to talk about it. She knew him well enough not to push.

"I found a button. It looks new. Did you find anything?"

"Not really." Stewart pointed up toward a hill where there was a fence and cows of a different breed than the Black Angus that Stewart owned. "The neighbor would have seen the lights from up there. That's some distance away, and the darkness would have distorted things. He might have been mistaken about it being close to the homestead."

"But for sure someone was out here?"

He took his hat off and ran his hands through his hair. "There's no reason for Randy to lie about that, but he is older, so maybe he wasn't seeing clearly."

"Someone walking around with a flashlight is pretty distinct. Is that what he said he saw, not headlights like someone who just parked out here or was driving through?"

"Yeah, he said it was a single bobbing light." Stewart stared at his cows grazing contentedly. "I don't like the idea of anyone's cows being stolen. Wish we could catch whoever was doing this."

There was a weariness in his voice, and she realized that he had probably gone without much sleep. He had still been working making calls while she napped. "Are you going to be able to get some rest before you have to go to work?"

He shrugged. "Probably not. Come on, I'll take you back home."

Stewart was silent for the entire drive back to the house. They stepped inside. Stewart glanced at the clock on the living room wall. "My deputy will be here in less than half an hour. I'm not sure about you being here alone."

"I'll be okay."

"Stay inside. Mom should be home before dark."

Though she understood that his motive was to protect her, it felt like he was ordering her around. Her oversensitive response probably had less to do with his directives and more to do with how going out to the old homestead had stirred up unbidden memories.

Being in the room with him wasn't helping anything. "I'm going to make myself a cup of tea. Do you want anything?"

He shook his head.

By the time she'd made her tea and stepped back into the empty living room, the deputy had pulled up outside.

Stewart emerged from the hallway. He'd changed into his uniform and was headed toward the door. "Call me if anything happens."

"I'll be okay." It was at least a twenty-minute drive from town to the ranch house. And Stewart could be called out to anywhere in the county.

He studied her for a moment. "I better get going."

Through the big front windows, she could see that his deputy had exited the car to stretch. "It's pretty safe out here," she said.

"I'll do a patrol through here if I can."

"Stewart, I know that you have a job to do. Don't worry about me. You don't have to come out here unless it's part of your duty."

He nodded and stepped out the door. He returned a moment later to hand her the new phone the deputy had brought.

She stood by the window watching as the sheriff's vehicle backed up and headed down the road.

She stared out at the vast expanse of land that surrounded the ranch house. His concern for her safety touched her. She suspected that if she had been a stranger, he would have had the same response. He was a good man who took his job seriously.

They had been in love once. The feelings that had been stirred up by visiting the homestead weren't about the present. They were about the past.

She didn't love him anymore. They were both different people from the eighteen-year-olds who'd planned a life together. Because of what had happened, they could never be that innocent again.

When Stewart's car disappeared over the hill, the silence of the house felt oppressive. Her heart beat a little faster. She turned the deadbolt on the front door and then went to confirm that the kitchen entrance was locked as well.

She hurried up the stairs to check the view from her bedroom as evening fell and a shroud of gray covered the sky.

After being called out on several minor calls and assisting highway patrol with an accident, Stewart phoned the house. The landline rang until it went to voice mail.

"Lila, it's Stewart. Just wanted to check in with you." He made a mental note that he needed to get her new cell number from her.

When he called his mother's cell, she did

not pick up either. He waited for the beep and left another message. "Just wondering if you made it back to the house."

His gut tightened as he grabbed his jacket and headed out to the sheriff's car. He tried to console himself that the panic he felt could be nothing. Lila might not have heard the phone ring. His mother might be in the studio with the music up loud.

Unless he got another call, he had time to drive out to the ranch house. Once he was outside the city limits, his headlights cut through the darkness. The drive gave him too much time to think.

Ever since he'd gone on shift, he'd been antsy. It felt like he could run a hundred miles without stopping. Though Lila's safety was foremost on his mind, that was not what had caused a lack of focus. Having Lila mention the times they had spent together at the old homestead and remembering the power of their first kiss had brought everything to the surface.

He was fine as long as he didn't have to talk about the past. Why did she bring it up?

When he came up over the hill, the house was dark. Lila's room was not visible from this angle. He parked and hurried up the porch. The door was locked. He pulled his key out, pushed the door open and stepped into the dark room. "Hello, Lila… Mom?"

His phone dinged that he had a text.

Mom telling him she'd been delayed because her friend was not feeling well.

Stewart's cowboy boots pounded the wood floor, seeming to echo in the silent house. He hurried up the stairs to Lila's room. Finding the door open, he peered inside. Empty.

By the time he headed back down the stairs, his heart was racing He rushed into the kitchen. The back door was unlocked. He opened it and stared out into the darkness.

In the distance, he heard the sound of a horse's pounding hooves, and then a woman screamed.

SIX

Lila screamed and climbed the fence as an Angus bull rushed toward her. A few minutes before when she looked out her window, she'd noticed that a horse was in the backyard and assumed it had gotten out of its corral. She'd gone outside to see if she could usher Houdini back to his corral only to find all three horses had escaped. While she'd led one horse back she was charged by the bull. And that horse had run off again.

Somewhere in the darkness, Stewart called her name.

"Over here." His timing could not have been better.

She swung her leg over the fence just as the bull butted it with his head. The force of the impact vibrated through her hand where she gripped the top of the fence. She jumped. Her feet squished down into the mud of the adjoining pen. The pig in the corner snorted and ambled toward her.

The bull butted the fence a second time, huffing and stomping the ground.

Stewart stepped closer to her. "What is that bull doing in that section of corral?"

"Being angry?" said Lila.

Stewart laughed. "He does have an attitude, which is why he's supposed to be sectioned off. Are you all right?"

"Relatively speaking." Her heart still pounded wildly.

"There's a cattle prod and flashlight in the barn just inside the door. Can you run and get it for me?" Stewart stood his ground by the angry bull but did not move toward it.

Lila climbed out of the pigpen and ran around to the barn entrance. The cattle prod hung on a hook, and the flashlight lay on the shelf just inside the door. She grabbed them and returned quickly, handing them to Stewart and then backing off from the bull.

"I'll go see if I can get the horses rounded up," she said.

"Give me a minute. I need to make sure this guy is back in solitary confinement."

Lila turned and spotted two of the horses standing in the front yard. She remembered seeing rope in the barn. The animals were still waiting for her when she returned. She looped the ropes and put it over their heads.

When she led the horses back toward the corral, Stewart was lifting fence beams in place. The black bull was barely visible at the far end of a different corral that Stewart had sectioned off.

Stewart moved to open a gate and then turned to face her. “You can bring them back in here.”

She tugged on the ropes, directing the horses through.

“Was this gate open when you came out here?”

“I’m not sure,” she said. “I kind of had other things on my mind.”

“I don’t know how Festus got out of his area.” Stewart pointed back toward the bull.

“Could he have knocked the fencing down?” she asked.

She knew from having helped Stewart years ago that this fencing was like sturdy Lincoln Logs, so a person could configure the corrals however they wanted.

Stewart picked the flashlight up where he’d rested it on a fence post and shone it on the beams he had just put back in place. He shook his head. “I don’t know. It seems like they would show some breakage if Festus barged through, then the horses would have jumped the fence to get away from him."

A chill ran down her spine. Had someone opened up the corral knowing she'd come out to rescue the horses and be charged by the bull when she tried to put them back in their section of the corral?

"Why don't you go inside the house, Lila?" Though he had not vocalized what she was thinking, an ominous tension threaded through his words.

"What about the other horse?"

"Gilbert will return on his own. He never goes far. He'll be waiting by the fence for morning feeding. I can guarantee you that."

She trudged toward the house, reaching for the kitchen door. She caught sight of Stewart just as he headed around the barn to put away the flashlight and the prod. She stood for a moment with her hand on the doorknob unable to shake the feeling that she was being watched.

Stewart returned the flashlight and the prod to the barn. His teeth were clenched so tight his jaw hurt. He hadn't wanted to alarm Lila, but he was pretty sure the sabotage to the fencing had not been done on accident or by a bull. It could have been messed with at any time today. There had been hours when no one was on the ranch grounds. How could someone know that Lila would be the one to run out to usher the horses back into their corral?

Everyone around here knew that Festus was a difficult animal who needed to be confined. If he wasn't such great breeding stock, Stewart would have gotten rid of him long ago.

He walked to the ranch house. Lila had taken her muddy shoes off at the door. She must be upstairs changing. He let his deputy know via radio where he was and that he would return soon. He poured himself a glass of water. Lila returned to the kitchen wearing different shoes and a clean pair of jeans.

"Sorry about tracking mud into your kitchen."

"Par for the course since you had to escape through the pigpen." He took a gulp of water and set the glass on the counter. His tone grew serious. "I can't have you stay here alone." Even if his mom did come back before the night was over, it wasn't like she could provide much protection if someone was getting so bold as to come onto the property.

"You think what happened out there was on purpose?"

"Nothing I can prove. Maybe Roy or Elliot

opened up that section for whatever reason and didn't make sure it was secure. I just can't take a chance. Why don't you come back to the sheriff's office with me?"

"I need to sleep, Stewart. How about I stay at my house? Can't one of your deputies be parked outside?"

"All I know is that I can't leave you here alone. Ride with me into town." The safest place for her would be in the sheriff's office, though it was hardly a place conducive to sleep.

She let out a breath. "I'll get my coat."

He was standing at the door waiting for her when she came down the stairs. She lifted the laptop case she was holding. "If I'm going to spend the night in the sheriff's office, I thought I might get some work done."

"Sorry to do this to you. There is a cot you can sleep on."

They both got into the sheriff's vehicle. Stewart had gotten turned around and was headed back toward town when the radio hissed.

He pressed the talk button. "Sheriff Duncan. What is it, Moira?"

The dispatcher's voice came across the line. "We got a call about spotting that stolen blue Jeep headed up Heeb Road toward the Franzen farm. Are you still close to the ranch house? That would be in your neck of the woods."

"I can check it out." Stewart did an abrupt turn when he came to the crossroads that led into town or deeper into farm country. He glanced at Lila and kept driving. "This is what I was concerned about. I don't want you going out on calls with me. It's not safe."

"I guess we have no choice. You have to do your job." Lila sat clutching her laptop.

He drove for several miles.

On the flat straight road, he caught sight of flashing hazard lights up ahead. As they drew nearer to the car, his headlights revealed that this car matched the description of the one that had been reported stolen days ago. The car door was flung open as though someone had fled quickly.

It had not been his intent that Lila would end up going out on a call with him, but he had been closer than his deputy. Protocol dictated that the nearest officer took the call. "You stay in the car."

Lila nodded as a look of weariness clouded her expression.

Well aware that whoever had abandoned the car might still be close, he pushed open the door after radioing the dispatcher where he was. His cowboy boots touched the rutted road, still muddy from the last rainfall. He drew his weapon and tuned into his surroundings. Wind rustled the budding leaves on the trees lining either side of the road. The most distinct sound, though, was the incessant dinging from the headlights being left on in the car with the door open.

Heart racing, he approached the car, pivoted and pointed his gun toward the empty driver's seat. He lifted his head and scanned the dark forest. Lila's face was visible through the windshield of the sheriff's car. She turned her head in the direction he had just looked.

Had the driver seen them coming and decided it was better to run on foot than be caught in the stolen car? Maybe he or she would have seen an approaching car on the straight road, but at night from a distance they would not have been able to tell it was a sheriff's car until it was closer. His best guess was that the car had been stolen by a teenager who got scared over the thought of being caught and had taken off running.

After pulling the flashlight off his belt, he circled around the car looking for footprints. He noticed a waffle pattern that might be a boot print leading off into the trees. It was too dark and far away to detect any movement if someone was hiding in the trees watching.

He pushed the talk button on his shoulder radio to let Moira know what he'd found. They would have to arrange for a tow back to the impound yard.

At the risk of the thief returning, Stewart would have to stay with the Jeep until the tow truck arrived. After turning off the headlights and closing the door on the stolen vehicle, he walked back to the sheriff's car, opened the door and explained the situation to Lila.

She stared at the ceiling. "That will take forever. Why don't I just drive the car back? I can follow you into town."

"There might be fingerprints or other evidence of who the thief was. Having you sit in the driver's seat would contaminate things."

"I guess we have no choice, then," she said.

When he got behind the wheel, he could sense the tension. Lila stared off into the distance, her mouth drawn into a tight line. He knew what it meant when she got that look on her face. She didn't want to talk. The idea that she was upset with him bothered him. Despite the hostility between them, he was trying to do the right thing.

"I just want you to be safe, okay? I don't want anyone getting hurt, or worse, on my watch. But I also have a job to do for the rest of the county."

"I can appreciate that, but I came back here to accomplish something too, Stewart."

"I know you need a phone and another rental car. I will see to it that that happens tomorrow."

"Between the ranch and the sheriff's job, you seem to have two full-time jobs and not much time to spare."

"I feel a debt to this community. That's why I ran for sheriff."

She looked directly at him. "It also proves to people that you aren't your father. That you are Mr. Law and Order. Don't you think that has something to do with it?"

Her comment felt like a punch to his gut. "Lila, let it go." They were both exhausted. He didn't want fatigue to cause him to say something he'd regret.

"I accept that you don't care about finding out what really happened, but I just hope the day comes when you learn not to always close the door on your feelings."

"What are you saying?" He regretted asking the question even before he was done with the sentence. He had the awful feeling he was about to step on an emotional land mine.

"I just think you're running yourself ragged

trying to prove you are a different man than your father. And you have probably been doing that since I left. Staying busy means you don't ever have to process the past. Between the ranch and this job, do you ever get a day off?" The tone of her voice had changed from accusatory to compassionate.

He opened his mouth to object but caught himself. Even after ten years, she knew him better than anyone. His father's bad acts had cast a dark shadow over his own life that he had been trying to step free of for a long time. "Guess I don't really get a day off. Things pile up at the ranch once I don't have to go into the sheriff's office."

"You can't say your current life isn't affected by the past," she said. "By who your father was and what he did."

Stewart gripped the steering wheel and then flexed his hands. He couldn't even process the emotion that made him tense up. It wasn't anger at Lila. Her intent was not to pick a fight, but to speak truth into his life, and that was what bothered him. His choices were driven by things that had happened years ago that he could not change. "You might be right about that, but what can I do?"

"For one thing you can quit working so hard and have a life."

"I have obligations, Lila."

"What do you do for fun, to relax?"

"I help coach the junior high football team."

"That sounds like another obligation to me," she said.

Why was she bringing this up?

"I know that I have added to your stress, and I'm sorry about that. But what I see is a man who has forgotten how to enjoy life, because he feels like he always has to be proving himself."

No one else would have spoken this truth to him in such a gentle way. "Maybe you're right." Lost in thought, he looked off through the side window, catching some movement in the trees. He pushed open the door. "Stay here."

Stewart pulled his weapon and ran across the road into the dark forest.

As he neared the trees, he heard more noise—someone or something moving through the forest.

"Police, stop."

He raised his gun and stepped in the direction the sounds had come from, though now the forest seemed to have fallen silent.

The hairs on the back of his neck stood at attention. Someone was close, watching him. The sound of his own breathing amplified in the quiet.

He took another step, his boot pressing against the ground. A sudden burst of movement off to his side caught his attention and he ran in that direction. Now he knew who he was chasing. The distinctive long blond hair was easy to see even at night. Leon Bellweather was a sixteen-year-old who had been in trouble before.

"Leon, stop!"

The kid kept running. Stewart pursued him as they both crashed through the trees, ducking branches and jumping over undergrowth.

After about five minutes, Leon slowed down and then halted, putting his hands in the air.

Stewart stepped forward and cuffed Leon's hands behind his back. "Car theft is a little more serious than the shoplifting."

"I didn't steal the car," said Leon.

"That's every criminal's story."

"I didn't. Someone offered me money to drive it around and watch until you showed up."

"Who?"

"I don't know. I never saw him or her. I just got texts. A hundred dollars was waiting for me in an envelope at the hotel where my mom works. The car was right where the person said it would be with the keys in it. I was promised more money if I did what the person said."

Stewart led Leon through the trees.

Leon's story seemed a far-fetched way to claim innocence. "And what were you supposed to do if I pulled up?"

"I was supposed to watch and text him if there was a woman with you in the car and then run away."

Stewart froze as a chill ran over his skin. "Hurry, we need to get back to that patrol car."

This was a setup. Lila was in danger.

SEVEN

The longer Lila sat in the car, the more afraid she became. There was something about being alone in the wilderness that made her feel vulnerable even under normal circumstances. She had to admit she felt safer when Stewart was around.

She'd locked the doors the second Stewart had gotten out. She stared at her hands resting on her laptop. Movement in her peripheral vision drew her attention to the side window.

An object was hurled at her, creating a spiderweb pattern in the glass.

She screamed and moved away, not fully comprehending what was happening.

It took two more blows to the window before it shattered. A man in a ski mask was beating the door with a stick. He reached in to undo the lock.

She crawled toward the driver's side door on her stomach and reached up to unlock it.

The man grabbed her by her legs and dragged her out.

Trees, ground and darkness whirled around her like a kaleidoscope. When she looked up, the sheriff's car seemed miles away as she was dragged deeper into the forest. Then all she saw were the trunks of trees.

The man had an arm clamped around her waist and the other over her mouth. She clawed at his hand, trying to force him to let go. He tightened his grip, pressing his arm into her stomach. His fingers squeezed into her cheeks where he covered her mouth. Her kicking and attempts at trying to twist free of his grip only made him hold her tighter.

After yanking her into the trees, he let go and pushed her to the ground. Because he was dressed all in black she could see only his eyes as he pulled a gun out of his belt. It shone in the moonlight when he aimed it at her.

She screamed.

"Lila," Stewart shouted.

The shooter looked off to the side where the voice came from and then took off running in the opposite direction from where Stewart was.

Stewart reached her. He knelt down. Concern etched across his features as his hand rested on her shoulder. “You okay?”

“He went that way.” She pointed.

Stewart rose to his feet and sprinted into the trees.

She moved to get up off the ground but collapsed onto the cold earth. Her heart was still pounding as shock sank in. Clutching her stomach, she angled to one side. She feared she might throw up.

A shot was fired, and a different gun replied deeper in the trees. She jerked, taking in a sharp breath.

Had Stewart been shot?

Still light-headed, she pushed herself to her feet.

Stewart emerged from the darkness. “I lost him. I think I know where he must have parked. Come on. We might be able to catch him.”

He led her back to the sheriff’s car. A blond teenager sat in the back seat.

In what was almost one swift motion, Stewart got behind the wheel and swept away the glass that was on her seat while she was still opening the door.

The shock had caused her to go numb.

Before she even had her seat belt on, Stewart pulled back onto the road and cranked the wheel to get turned around.

They sped up the road. The SUV shook back and forth from the bogginess of the mud.

Headlights glared at them up ahead, the tow truck.

On the single lane road, Stewart swerved around the tow truck bumping along in the grass.

The blond teenager spoke up. “I’ve never been in a high-speed chase before.”

Stewart took an abrupt turn into the forest. They were on a road that was nothing more than two ruts. He ran over brush and then took another turn. The opening between the trees was so narrow that branches brushed the metal body of the car. Lila dug her fingers into the armrest.

After lurching over several bumps, they came out on a smoother road, and Stewart sped up. They drove for several minutes on a curvy dirt road without seeing any taillights or sign of another car.

Stewart slowed down. “I lost him.” He looked at Lila. “I don’t suppose you can identify him?”

His frustration was palpable.

“He wore a ski mask,” she said.

Stewart let out an audible breath. He

phoned the tow truck driver and let him know what happened and that he would meet him at the sheriff's office, and then drove back out to a paved road.

He lifted his chin and spoke to the teenager in the back seat. "Leon, you have some questions to answer for me."

"I know, sir," said Leon. "I'm sorry for all the trouble."

She wasn't sure what was going on, but it appeared that the young man named Leon must somehow be connected to what had just happened. Whatever Leon had done, he seemed to have enormous respect for Stewart.

She thought about what she had said to Stewart earlier, that his workaholism was driven by his need to prove himself over and over. Though she still believed it was true, there was a part of her that admired what Stewart had. He was a respected part of this community. Maybe she had belonged at one time but not anymore. She was the outsider.

Despite her success, Seattle had never felt like home. The only place she had ever felt a sense of belonging was in Trident.

They came to the edge of town. At this hour, Main Street was mostly shut down. Stewart drove to the sheriff's office. He parked in the back parking lot and turned to face her.

"If you want to come inside, I'll deal with Leon and write up a report about what happened. I'll need to talk to you as well."

Several streetlamps illuminated the parking lot as He escorted Leon inside, and she trailed behind. Stewart took the boy into a room down a hallway that must be an interview room. The place had three desks. The jail cells may have been in a different part of tho building.

Lila sat down on a bench by the door after putting her laptop to one side. Within minutes, she could feel herself about to nod off. She closed her eyes and gave in to exhaustion.

She didn't know how much time had passed when Stewart shook her shoulder. Her face rested on the laptop cover.

"Lila, come on. Wake up."

She jerked awake and sat up, smoothing over her hair. "Wow, I must be really tired."

Deputy Swain sat at one of the desks.

Stewart gazed down at her. His smile warmed her heart. "I'll walk you to your house so you can get some sleep."

"Do you think that will be safe?"

"I'm going to crash on the couch if that's okay with you." He tilted his head toward the deputy. "I called in some extra help. I'm taking this day off."

So what she'd said had meant something to him. She glanced at the clock on the wall. Two in the morning.

She rose and followed him outside. They walked down a quiet street that contained older Victorian houses that had been turned into businesses. They passed a lawyer's office, a custom printing place and a photography studio.

"What happened to Leon?"

"I let him go. He was set up to lure us out there. There are a few leads I need to follow, but Leon doesn't really know anything."

They turned onto the street that led to her old house, which was set apart because of the large lot. The windows in the houses they passed were all dark.

The stillness of the town at this hour comforted her. They arrived at her house, and she opened the door.

The memory of the previous assault here and then the man in the ski mask dragging her into the forest to kill her hit her with such an intense force that she froze on the threshold. They must be the same person.

Stewart rubbed her shoulder. "Let me check the place out. Come inside and stay by the door." He stepped around her and headed toward the kitchen.

Lila closed the door and locked the deadbolt. She appreciated that she did not have to explain why she'd been unable to step inside. He seemed to understand.

She could hear his boots on the wooden floor as he headed down the hallway to her old room.

He returned. "I'll look upstairs too."

"Let me grab you a pillow and some blankets." She hurried down a hallway to a well-stocked linen closet, thanks to the property manager. She stepped into the living room just as Stewart came down the stairs.

Though they might have been followed, there was no way the attacker could have known they were going to come to the house and been waiting for them. The gesture was a kindness on Stewart's part to make her feel safer.

She handed him the blanket. "I'm glad you're taking the day off."

"A very wise friend suggested I should." His gaze was unwavering as he stared at her with warmth in his eyes.

Her heart fluttered when he looked at her. "I'm glad you see me as a friend."

Grateful that something in their relationship had been mended, she pivoted and headed toward the hallway. When she looked back at Stewart, he was moving from window to window, probably looking for anything suspicious. A reminder that, so far, no place had been entirely safe for her.

Lila trudged up the hall, crawled under the lush covers and fell asleep almost immediately.

The sun warming his face awakened Stewart. He opened his eyes and sat up, surprised at how well he'd slept. Exhaustion and stress tended to do that.

A sudden fear that he had slept through something bad happening to Lila caused him to bolt to his feet. He hurried down the hall. When he peered through the half-open door, he breathed a sigh of relief. Lila slept underneath a blue comforter.

He returned to the living room. After folding his blanket and placing the pillow on it, he ambled into the kitchen. The place was set up as a B and B. Maybe there was something to eat. He found coffee in a cupboard and creamer and sugar on the counter beside the coffee maker.

He set up a pot to brew and then went to the powder room to splash water on his face.

He caught a glimpse of himself in the mirror. He wondered if Lila had noticed the encroaching worry lines on his forehead. Was that why she'd pointed out that he was working too much?

The prospect of a day off made him feel a little lost. He half hoped he would be called in for an emergency at the ranch or sheriff's office.

As he entered the kitchen, he glanced up the hallway where Lila was standing. She still wore her clothes from yesterday. "I smelled the coffee."

"I'll get you a cup. It should be done by now."

He poured the coffee, and she stepped into the kitchen and stood a few feet from him. He was keenly aware of her proximity as he scooped the sugar and stirred it in her cup.

"You remember that I liked two teaspoons of sugar," she said.

He remembered a lot of things about her. He lifted the cup, turning it so she could grab the handle. Flashes of memory, images, flowed through his mind. He could picture that pensive look she got when she was drawing or painting.

Lila turned to look out the kitchen window as she took her first sip of coffee. He poured himself a cup, shaking his head as another memory floated to the surface: watching Lila from a distance as she picked wildflowers. They'd gone for a horseback ride. Then he saw a snapshot of her face when he proposed after they had hiked to the top of Bear Canyon.

His smile faded. The next picture that came into his head caused a sour taste in his mouth. The wedding invitations they'd been filling out together had sat for a full six months gathering dust at the ranch house before his mother kindly packed them away. It took him over a year to accept that Lila wasn't coming back.

She looked at him. "Are you okay? You look…upset."

He shook his head and turned away. Lila could read him like a book. He didn't want that scrutiny right now. And he sure didn't want to talk about the jumbled, contradictory images in his head. "Just thinking."

He was grateful to hear his phone ringing in the living room. He picked it up. The number was his deputy. Maybe he wasn't going to have a day off. If that was the case, part of him was grateful given how being around Lila brought unwanted turmoil to the surface.

"Deputy Swain. What is it?"

Lila stood in the doorway between the kitchen and the living room leaning against the frame and sipping her coffee.

"I know it's your day off, but I thought you might want to know. The FBI notified this office that they are done combing the area around where the getaway car was found."

"Thank you for letting me know." If they had found anything significant, they would have released that information to him. "Did they say if they were going to reopen the case?"

"Haven't heard yet," said Deputy Swain.

The Bureau would do their job. His focus needed to be on the current attacks on Lila, not on what had happened ten years ago. "Did you have time to look for prints on the stolen car?"

"Just Leon's prints, which means whoever actually stole it wiped everything down."

"A lot of planning went into that," said Stewart. "I wonder if anyone saw the car being dropped off before Leon picked it up."

"With all due respect, sir, this is your day off. We have things well in hand. Enjoy yourself. I just thought you might want to know about the FBI being done."

"If you're sure everything is okay there?"

"Just peachy. Sir, your idea of taking a day off was a good one."

Swain's remark surprised him. "Really?"

"You're a great sheriff, a good rancher and an excellent assistant coach for junior high football. In the years I've known you, I don't recall you ever taking a personal day for anything. Something must have changed for the better."

Stewart caught a glimpse of Lila as she wandered back into the kitchen. She'd had the courage to point out what everyone else must have seen. "Look, can I borrow one of your cars? I don't think it would be appropriate to use the sheriff's vehicle."

"Sure, no problem. Swing by. You know where I keep the keys. What do you need it for?"

"I need to help a friend."

"Take care," said Deputy Swain.

Stewart turned his phone off then poked his head into the kitchen. "How about I take you to go get that rental car?"

"That sounds good."

"The FBI is done in the area where they found the car. If you want, we can go there first and get the car on the way back."

"I'd appreciate that." Her demeanor brightened at his offer.

Lila wasn't going to find anything at the scene where the car had been found that the FBI had missed. His hope was that it would give her some sense of closure so she would let go of the idea that she could solve the case the police couldn't. He thought too that maybe if he could convince her to return to Seattle the attacks on her would stop.

He had mixed feelings about spending the day with her. Being around her reminded him not only of the innocent love they had once had for each other but also the deep hurt. They seemed to have come to a sort of truce, an agreement to treat each other as friends, and that was good.

"Give me a minute to call the ranch and let them know where I'll be," he said.

"I'll get freshened up." Lila hurried down the hall to the other bathroom.

He called and Roy picked up. Stewart explained where he would be for the rest of the day and ended the call by saying, "If there's anything you and Elliot can't handle or have questions about, I'm a phone call away."

"Will do," said Roy.

Lila returned and handed him a plastic package. "The main bathroom is stocked with toiletry kits, in case you want to brush your teeth."

"Thank you."

Within a few minutes, they were ready to leave. Once they were outside, Lila shook the door handle to make sure it was locked. "Thanks for getting that fixed."

Tension coiled inside him as Stewart scanned the street. Lila edged a little closer while they walked toward the sheriff's vehicle.

Her actions indicated that she too was fully aware that another attempt on her life could happen at any time.

EIGHT

After trading out the sheriff's vehicle for the deputy's personal car, Lila and Stewart grabbed a quick bite at a food truck that sold breakfast burritos. The place where the getaway car was found was about fifty miles from town.

Lila had read the newspaper accounts of the robbery at least half a dozen times. Evidence suggested that her father had let Stewart's father in after the bank closed. There was no sign of forced entry. No money was taken from teller drawers. Three safe-deposit boxes had been drilled and cleaned out. Again, it appeared that there was insider knowledge about which boxes had the most valuable items.

She knew from having worked at the bank that even though the bank employee had the second key that opened the boxes, the owner of the box was always given an area closed off by a curtain to place or take things out of the box.

Police had speculated that because her father had known the balance of clients' bank accounts that he targeted the boxes most likely to reap a substantial reward. The gossip around town after the robbery was that her father had drew it out of people through conversation as to what was in the boxes. Plus her father would have known the bank balances of people, who had money and who didn't. The problem was none of that fit with who her father was.

One of the things that had driven her away from Trident was how quickly so many in the town had assumed her father's guilt once he disappeared.

Stewart slowed down as he rounded a curve on the highway. The change in speed drew her back into reality. She had been so lost in thought, she had failed to notice the mountains in the distance and the evergreens that lined the road.

Here she was in a car on a beautiful day with the man she had once thought she would spend her life with.

"Penny for your thoughts," he said.

"Can you guess?"

He smiled and shook his head. "I probably shouldn't ask."

"I can't let it go, Stewart."

"I get that. Maybe someday you will be able to."

His last comment felt a little like a barb. The only way she'd be able to let go was if she knew the truth of what had happened that day. Though she still felt a chasm between them that probably would never be healed, it seemed that they had come to a sort of peace. He was being gracious taking her to where the car had been found.

A sign read that a picnic area was five miles away. That was where the car had been found.

"It's weird that the car remained hidden all these years," she said.

"It was parked close to the river. A short time after the robbery, there were heavy rains that caused the riverbank to rise. There was a mudslide that partially covered the car. It could be that people saw the car and didn't make the connection to the robbery."

He turned into the recreational area. They passed a small gravel parking lot and some picnic tables. He drove a little farther to where the riverbed was level with the land. He parked the car facing the river.

Lila felt a chill rush over her skin as she stared out at the drag marks and the hole where the car must have been pulled out. She pushed open the door. The breeze ruffled her hair when she walked toward where the car had been. The car had belonged to her father. One more thing that had cemented his guilt in everyone's eyes.

When the news story had first surfaced, the photographs of the rusting dilapidated car had caused her to double over. She remembered praying, asking God to please let this be the evidence that gave her the closure she longed for.

"Did the FBI find anything significant?"

Stewart shook his head. "Water and time destroyed most everything. It was long shot."

Though it had been the thing that had made her finally return to Trident, it didn't sound like much evidence had been found beyond the car itself.

She walked past the drag marks to where the ground was sunken it. It wasn't a dead end. Her return had caused someone to be willing to kill in order to keep her from snooping around. That had to matter to the cold case investigation.

The detective she'd hired years ago hadn't elicited this kind of reaction. As she stared at the hole where the car had been, she felt her resolve growing. Her return had caused a culprit to surface. Maybe someone who had been involved in the robbery or someone with something to hide or someone to protect.

She walked a little way down the riverbank listening to the sound of the water lapping against the shore. She stopped and crossed her arms, staring out at the flowing water. When she looked down closer to the shore a pretty rock in the water caught her attention. Anytime she made a resolution to see something through to the end, she made a habit of collecting an item that would remind her of that decision. When she'd been in Seattle, the decision to succeed as an artist had been made outside a thrift store. She entered the store and bought a teacup that sat on her shelf to remind her of the goal. Every time she had a setback, she would look at that cup and persist in making her dream happen.

She reached down to pick up the stone. Cold water rushed around her hand.

The green stone was pretty and different from all those around it.

"Find something?" Stewart had stepped closer to her.

She turned to face him with an open palm. "To remind me of a decision I made."

"Which is?"

"I'm not leaving here until I find out what happened to my father."

The softness of Stewart's expression transformed into all angles and hard edges. "I think you would be safer in Seattle. It's clear you have stirred something up. Let me handle this."

Lila clenched her teeth to keep from saying something she would regret. Just like he'd been *handling* it for the last ten years.

"I don't want something bad to happen to you, Lila." His voice was filled with anguish.

The intensity of his words caught her off guard. It seemed as if his response had less to do with his duty as sheriff and more that he cared about her. She saw how bent out of shape he was. She was not going to go another round with him having the same old fight. "I've made my decision." Her words were barely above a whisper. "It's my presence in this town that has moved the case forward."

"There is no need for you to make yourself a target."

"I appreciate so much that you care about what happens to me. I don't want to take up the sheriff's department resources. Maybe I can look into hiring some professional security."

"This is a small town, Lila. The closest

you will get to private security is the karate instructor."

"So I'll hire him. I'm not trying to make your life harder, Stewart. I really am not."

He angled sideways and stared at the pebbles on the beach. "I don't know what to say anymore."

Say you'll support me. Say you want to find out the truth. "Maybe we should just go get my rental car. That was the plan, right?"

He nodded and turned away.

Lila let out a heavy breath and followed Stewart back to the car.

Once they were in the car, Stewart turned on the radio. The music gave him an excuse not to have to talk. He couldn't believe how stubborn she was. Whatever closeness he'd felt to her when they'd had coffee was too fragile to last.

As he pulled out onto the road, he noticed a black truck parked in the picnic area.

Lila remained quiet as well, staring out the window or at the rock she'd picked up.

By the time the signs for the airport's car rental place appeared, the sky had turned gray. More rain.

After two drought years, he should be grateful.

He pulled into the parking lot.

"I'll just run in and sign the paperwork and get the keys." She spoke as she unbuckled her seat belt.

"I'll wait for you and follow you back into town."

"Thank you. I do appreciate it."

The warmth of her words just caused him more turmoil. If only they hadn't loved each other so deeply once. This would be so much easier.

"I've got to go that way anyhow." He tried to sound lighthearted.

She laughed.

Her laughter pulled at his heartstrings. Being around her was such a roller-coaster ride.

She pushed the door open and went inside. Returning a few minutes later, she pointed toward a white compact car. He waited for her to pull out onto the street and slipped in behind her. By the time they got out to the highway, it was raining.

He focused on the road while making sure he could see her taillights. He tensed when a car pulled in behind Lila. A moment later, the car eased into the right lane and roared ahead of her. When he checked the rearview mirror, there were several cars behind him.

The rain came down harder and faster,

obscuring his view. The image through the windshield was murky. A pick-up truck passed him and got between him and Lila.

They turned off the highway onto the two lane that led into town. Just before the road grew curvy, the truck that was between them got into the right lane and sped up.

Stewart took the curves at a safe speed. He lost sight of Lila. He pressed the accelerator. The road straightened out. His chest squeezed tight. He still didn't see her.

On the side of the road, a place where the brush had been flattened caught his eye. He was going too fast to safely stop. He pulled over onto a shoulder, checked to see there was no oncoming traffic and turned around.

He passed the place where the brush had been flattened more slowly. He could see the back side of Lila's car where it had gone off the road. He pulled over, ran across the road and down the incline where her car was.

When he looked inside the driver's side window, Lila was slumped forward, not moving. He pulled his phone out as he opened her door. He touched her neck, letting out a breath when he felt her pulse. Blood trickled from her forehead.

A woman's voice came across the line. "What's your emergency?"

"Moira, this is Sheriff Duncan. I'm going to need an ambulance. A woman has been in a crash. I am on the two-lane leading into Trident about three miles from town."

"We'll be there as fast as we can, Sheriff." There was a stutter in the woman's voice. "Hopefully everything will be okay."

"Thank you." He disconnected the call. He reached in and touched Lila's hair just above where the cut was. Seeing her face so lifeless and drained of color sent shock waves through him. He vowed that even if the hurt from the past wasn't going to heal, he would keep her safe regardless of his emotional turmoil.

It meant a great deal to her to find out what had happened to her father. For that reason, he would quit thinking that her leaving town was the answer. He would support her in finding out the truth.

Stewart stared up the long, straight road. A truck was approaching from the direction they had been traveling. His spine straightened. Though it was still some distance away, it was the same color as the truck that had passed him and had been driving at high speeds. Was this the vehicle that had run Lila off the road? Was he coming back to make sure he'd finished the job?

He couldn't take any chances. Even though he was concerned about a back injury in moving Lila, he couldn't risk her being attacked again. Getting her to the safety of his car and out of there was the priority. He unclicked her seat belt. Glancing over his shoulder, he saw that the black truck was slowing down.

He gathered Lila into his arms and lifted her up.

The truck was getting closer. He wasn't going to make it to his car before the driver arrived, and even then, he might decide to ram into Stewart's borrowed car.

Grateful that Lila was light as a feather, he hurried into the trees to find a hiding place. That way the man would have to come after them on foot, and Stewart would have a better chance of stopping him and taking him into custody.

As Stewart rushed into the forest, he prayed that would be the outcome and he could keep Lila safe from harm.

NINE

Stewart heard the truck coming to a stop as he searched for a hiding place for Lila. When he laid her down behind some thick brush, she still had not regained consciousness.

A car door slammed, and then he heard the sound of boots coming into the wooded area. Stewart's heart pounded. When he was off duty, he did not carry a gun. If he could catch the man by surprise, he'd be able to take him down.

The footsteps were far apart which meant the man was searching for where they might have gone, probably looking in all directions. Crouching, Stewart moved slowly away from Lila. He didn't want her to be vulnerable. When he was several yards from where she rested, he peered above the brush.

He could see the man from behind as well as the gun he had in his hand. From his stance and his build, he looked to be a younger man, maybe in his mid to late twenties. Odd, that would have made him a teenager ten years ago.

Stewart moved in a little closer, taking cover behind a tree. The man didn't turn so Stewart could see his face, but with his back to Stewart, he thought he might be able to jump the man and get the gun away.

The shrill of the ambulance siren reached his ears. The man took off running back toward the road. Stewart chased after him. Before he reached the edge of the trees, he heard the truck roar away. Stewart stepped onto the road and pulled his phone out. The black truck was headed away from Trident. He called his deputy with the color and model of the truck. At least he'd gotten a good look at it. Deputy Swain promised to notify highway patrol. Maybe they would catch the guy.

As the ambulance drew closer, Stewart stood by Lila's rental car where he could be seen. The ambulance came to a stop, and two EMTs jumped out.

"This way," said Stewart. "She's back here in the trees."

One of the EMTs retrieved a stretcher while the other, John, came alongside Stewart. Stewart had coached him in football years ago. They headed into the trees.

"Was she thrown from the car, Sheriff?"

"No," said Stewart. "Long story. No time to explain. Let's just get her to the hospital and make sure she's okay."

The other EMT caught up with them. Stewart watched as they loaded Lila onto the stretcher.

"I'll follow you in my car," said Stewart.

Stewart got into the car he'd borrowed from his deputy and slipped behind the ambulance.

Praying as he drove, *Please, God, let her be okay.*

Lila awoke in a room that smelled like disinfectant. White sheets. White walls. She must be in the hospital. The gown she was wearing confirmed her theory about where she was. Her last memory was of a black truck bumping her from behind. And then coming beside her and forcing her off the road. After that, trees and greenery had filled the windshield, and then her world had gone dark.

The images the memory provoked caused her to take in a sharp breath. In every way, it felt like she was hanging on to the end of a rope with one hand. Though still determined to stay until she had answers, she wasn't sure if she had the emotional and physical strength to continue.

She closed her eyes and prayed.

God, please help me.

She was stiff and sore, and there was a bandage on her head. She heard voices in the hallway; Stewart was talking to someone. She pushed herself to a sitting position with much effort and pain.

The voices faded.

A moment later, Stewart stuck his head in the door. "You're awake."

"Barely," she said. "Tell me I don't have any broken bones."

"You were fortunate. Bruises and scrapes."

She touched her forehead where the bandage was.

"Some external damage," he said. "You were unconscious. The doctor is worried about a concussion."

Something about Stewart seemed different. He seemed less defensive, softer toward her.

"So, I can get checked out, right?" she said.

He nodded and stepped into the room, removing his cowboy hat. He stared at the floor. "Look, I owe you an apology."

"For what?"

Her heart skipped a beat when he met her gaze. She saw warmth in his eyes, maybe even affection.

"For trying to push you to leave town. I

guess I thought…" He shook his head. "I'm not sure what I thought. That if you left, I could go on pretending that the past could stay in the past. I was living a lie. What happened between our fathers matters enough for someone to hurt you, and I didn't respect your determination to get answers."

Her throat went tight, and her eyes warmed with tears. "Thank you, Stewart."

"When I saw you there in that car—" his voice faltered "—and you weren't moving…" He shook his head and took a step back as though he were trying to get the image out of his head. "I don't want my stubbornness to be the reason you end up dead."

A tear flowed down her cheek. Just when she was ready to give up, God had answered her prayer. She had Stewart's support.

"Stay in town as long as you need to. I will help as much as I can."

Lila could not find the words to respond to what he was saying. Instead, she held her hand out. He grabbed it and squeezed it. The strength of his grip renewed her resolve.

"I'm going to try to take time off from being Sheriff as much as possible to help you and keep you safe. There will still be ranch stuff to deal with. You can't call in sick to a farm."

"I understand." Knowing that Stewart was on her side eased her physical pain and lifted her spirits in a way that nothing else could.

"Why don't I go talk to the nurse and see about getting you checked out?"

"Sounds good, I'll get dressed." She glanced around the room. "I assume the medical staff left my clothes around here somewhere." She noticed a plastic bag resting on a chair. She moved to get out of bed but stopped when pain shot through her legs.

"I'll go get the nurse to help you get out of bed." Stewart left the room.

A moment later, a nurse with steel gray hair and a bounce in her step entered the room. "Hello, dear. We're finalizing the paperwork to get you checked out. Sheriff Duncan thought you might need some help."

"I'm just a little sore," said Lila.

The nurse put down the railing on the bed as Lila pulled back the covers. Her legs had bruises on them, but the biggest source of pain was across her chest and stomach where the seat belt had dug into her. The angle of impact from the other car must have been in such a way that the airbag had not deployed.

After she swung her legs around, the nurse helped her to the bathroom where she got dressed. Stewart was waiting for her in the lounge by the nurses' station when she came out.

"What now?"

"How about I take you back home? Nurse said you should rest. I sent my brother out to get your rental car. He said it still runs, but it's pretty scratched up."

"I'll have to report that to the rental company. Probably involves filing some sort of insurance claim. After two cars being sabotaged, I doubt I am the rental company's favorite person."

Stewart started to walk down the hall. She fell in beside him. She noticed he slowed down when she couldn't keep up.

"I might have a lead on who the man in the truck was. I saw him from the back."

"Really."

"Yes, his build and movement suggested someone our age or close to it, not an older guy at least."

"That would mean if he's the man behind all this, he would have been in high school or just a little older ten years ago."

She couldn't think of who it could be. Who close to their age would have had a connection to either Stewart's father or hers? Her father had hired high school boys to do work around the house, and he might even have hired someone to help out in the bank.

Stewart held the door open for her as they stepped out into the late-day sunshine. She was grateful it had stopped raining.

"The truck was headed away from town when I saw it. I phoned in a description, but so far no sighting by highway patrol."

"I'm sure he would have found a hiding place if he thought he might get caught." She opened her car door. Sitting down caused some pain. She cautiously pulled the seat belt across her lap knowing that it would hurt once it was secure. "Resting for the afternoon might be a good idea."

Once they were on the street, she asked, "Did your father hire someone close to our age to help at the ranch? Someone that maybe got wind of the robbery or was brought in to help."

"Not that I remember. My father had to do everything on the cheap. Roy didn't expect a lot beyond room and board and some cash, and my brother and I worked for free." Stewart drove through town. "If you don't mind, I just need to make a quick stop and pick up some things from the hardware store. You want to come in with me?"

Anything to get out of the seat belt.

She followed him onto the sidewalk. The hardware store was right next to an insurance sales office. The man sitting in the insurance office waved at them and then got up.

Lila assumed he was waving at Stewart, so she was surprised when he opened his door and looked at her.

She remembered the man from ten years ago. Adam Ferguson must be past sixty. He had been selling insurance in Trident forever.

He nodded at Stewart and then turned toward Lila. "I heard you were back in town."

"You probably also know why," she said.

"I was hoping I'd run into you. I haven't thought about that robbery in years. When I saw that article about the car, it reminded me of something."

Stewart glanced up and down the street. Maybe being out in the open was making him nervous. Would someone take a shot at her while they stood on a public street?

"What are you talking about, Adam?" As he spoke, Stewart put a protective hand on her upper back.

"I know that three safe-deposit boxes were targeted and drilled," Adam said.

The articles at the time of the robbery had not listed who owned those boxes for privacy reasons.

Adam continued, "There were only two insurance outfits in town back then, me and Les Smith. The two of us got to talking one night years ago. To the best of our knowledge only one guy filed a claim."

"The other two people could have been insured with someone in a different town," said Stewart.

Adam nodded. "That could be, but I doubt it. Your father was a real nice man, Lila. I would like for you to get some answers."

Adam was probably one of the few people who thought her father was innocent. Maybe there had been others, and they had been silenced by those so willing to point fingers and gossip.

"At the time, I didn't think it was ethical to say anything 'cause the guy was my client, but he's been dead for years. His name was Charles Inman."

"I don't suppose you could tell us what he had in that box?"

"I don't want to cross a line here. His widow still lives on the ranch he bought. You should talk to her."

Stewart thanked Adam and ushered Lila into the hardware store. As Stewart grabbed some cording and a hammer, Lila's head buzzed with the information. Was it possible that the other two safe-deposit boxes had been decoys to throw the police off? Certainly, the FBI must have spoken to the other two people even if their names had not been public information.

Stewart remained quiet as they made their way up another aisle where he grabbed some bolts.

"Do you think what Adam said is important?"

He leaned close and answered in a nervous whisper, "Let's not talk about it out in the open."

The information had clearly set Stewart on edge.

TEN

Stewart's primary concern was getting Lila home safe. Talking about the case where people might hear felt like a bad idea. As he ushered her toward the counter so he could pay for the items he'd picked up, his stomach tightened at the thought of more harm coming to her. He shot a glance at Lila after he pulled out his wallet.

They stepped onto the street and got into his borrowed car. As he pulled out of the parking space and rolled through one of two lights, he found himself on high alert. The culprit seemed to favor cars as a weapon. He'd feel better when they were back at the ranch.

He'd made a vow to help her, and he intended to keep it. "It wouldn't hurt to talk to Charlie's widow and find out what she knows, but first you need to rest."

"I can't argue with you there," said Lila.

When they arrived at the ranch, his mother's car was parked close to the house, as was Lila's rental car. They stepped inside. The place smelled like fresh baked bread.

"Mom must be stuck with one of her projects. She always bakes when she gets artist's block."

"Smells nice," Lila said.

They found Cindy in the kitchen pulling a pan out of the oven. She smiled. "Just in time for hot rolls. They taste great with some melted butter."

In addition to the rolls, he saw a pile of chocolate chip cookies and a loaf of bread on the counter. His mother must really be in an inspiration rut.

Stewart grabbed a roll and split it open, taking in the sweet aroma. He handed one to Lila as well.

"Stewart says you bake when you can't figure something out with one of your projects," said Lila.

"My son knows me pretty well." His mother pushed the butter toward him, giving him a steely look.

Though his mom had been nothing but gracious toward Lila, he knew she felt protective of him. He'd been an emotional mess after Lila left. She just didn't want to see that happen again. It wasn't like he'd given away some big secret about his mom's habits as an artist.

"I know when I'm stuck, I weed my garden." Lila buttered her roll. "What are you working on?"

"A horse sculpture, actually three horses together. I've done a dozen sketches and roughed it out in clay, but it's still not working for me."

"I'd love to see what you have so far," said Lila. "Maybe I can help?"

His mother didn't answer right away. Instead, she took the pan of rolls back to the counter.

Lila was clearly trying to mend something between the two women. It wasn't his place to step in.

His mom turned back around. "That would be nice. I could use your keen eye for composition."

Stewart let out the breath he'd been holding. "I've got a fence to mend."

The sound of the two women chatting about art stuff was music to his ears as he headed toward the corral where the horses had gotten out and the bull had come after Lila.

He looked at the top horizontal piece that had broken. Now that he could see it in the daylight, it was clear what had happened. Part of the wood was smooth, like it had been partially sawed and then hit with something heavy to make it look like a break.

The thought that someone would come on the property and cause such sabotage was disturbing. They hadn't been bold enough to go inside and go after Lila. She'd probably locked all the doors, so they needed a way to get her to leave the house.

Once Lila had been lured outside, she would have been vulnerable to being attacked even if she did get away from the bull. There was no safe place for her. The only thing that would end this would be catching whoever was behind it.

He replaced the horizontal piece of wood on the fence and took his tools back to the barn. When he stepped outside, he glanced up on the ridge at a road leading to a neighboring farm. A black truck rolled by going slower than necessary.

His heart beat a little faster. That looked like the same black truck that had run Lila off the road. Stewart sprinted toward his car, jumped in and tore through the yard headed toward where the other truck had gone.

Instead of taking the curving road that led to the ridge, he drove sideways up the hill to cut out some time. He reached the gravel road where he'd seen the other truck and pressed down on the accelerator.

With gravel roads, there was a danger of going too fast. The rocks would act like marbles causing the vehicle to flip. He didn't see the other truck anywhere, but he kept going. The road curved and went up and down several hills and past two farms.

An older model Crown Victoria going in the other direction whizzed by him. The man waved as he went past by lifting two fingers off the steering wheel. A gesture known as the famous Montana wave.

Stewart knew the man. Kurt had moved to Trident several years ago to start an organic farm that was just up the road.

Stewart drove for only a few minutes more. He could see much of the road, and there was no sign of the black truck. This part of the county was dotted with farms and even some subdivisions. Catching the guy was an act of futility at this point.

A thought occurred to him, and he spun around in the road and headed toward Kurt's farm. Kurt was just getting out of his car as Stewart pulled into his driveway. The farmer carried what looked like flats of tomato plants from his car.

"Hey ya, Sheriff. Out of uniform today, huh?"

Stewart didn't feel the need to explain about taking a few days off. "Listen, Kurt, did a black truck go past you headed north maybe a few minutes before you saw me?"

"Matter a fact it did. The guy nearly ran me off the road."

"I don't suppose you got a look at him or his license plate?"

Kurt chuckled. "No, I was kind of worried about dying at the moment." He set the flat of plants on the hood of the car. "I did notice one thing as he was coming toward me. It looked like one of his headlights was bashed in."

"Thanks, Kurt." Stewart strode back to his car and got in. A bashed-in headlight could be fixed. He'd have to phone his deputies and let them know right away. The damage to the front of the truck did suggest it was probably the same vehicle that had run Lila off the road. If they could track down the truck, they'd no doubt find paint from Lila's car on it.

Stewart drove home more slowly, choosing the road instead of the cross-country route. Despite taking a deep breath, he couldn't loosen up the tension in his chest. The ranch was being watched. How long would it be before the culprit got bold enough to come inside the house for Lila?

He phoned his deputy to give him the new detail about the truck and the general direction it had been headed. Not a lot to go on.

After arriving at the house, he stepped inside. As soon as he came into the living room, he heard the laughter of the two women and smelled Italian spices. He found them both in the kitchen. His mom was stirring something on the stove, and Lila was setting the table.

Lila and his mother seemed to have mended their relationship. He thought back to a time when his life had been close to picture-perfect. Lila and Mom had gotten along so well, mostly because of their love for art.

Lila looked up from the table. "We've got some spaghetti on. Your little brother and his family can't make it, but Roy will be over in a few minutes."

His mom opened the oven and pulled out some garlic toast just as Roy stepped through the back door. The skin seemed to hang on his face, and his walk was heavy with fatigue.

"Long day?"

Roy nodded. "Looking forward to hitting the hay early. I hunted down three more heifers that are about to calf. They're in the pole barn out back. Elliot can come in and take the early shift, I can check on them through the night."

"Thanks." The time he had taken to help Lila meant that his brother and Roy bore more of the load in running the ranch. Because the ranch could not fully support him, Elliot had a second part-time job in town.

The tone of Roy's voice indicated he didn't like the extra workload.

"Why don't I help out?" asked Stewart's mom. "Since you and Lila have so much on your plate. Roy, if those calves aren't born tonight, I can look in on them in the early morning hours."

"Thanks, ma'am, I 'preciate it."

They sat down to their meal. After Stewart said grace, they passed around the bread, spaghetti and salad. "Lila, I thought you were going to take a nap." Visiting with his mom seemed to have energized her.

"I don't feel so tired anymore. Your mother gave me some ibuprofen for the soreness. I'm anxious to get over to talk to Charlie Inman's widow." Lila took a bite of bread. "We can still get that done today, can't we?"

Stewart had initially thought he would go there by himself. Now he wasn't so sure about leaving Lila at the ranch even if his mom was in the house and Roy was close by. "Yes, we can do that." He wasn't going to add to her fear by telling her about seeing the black truck.

His mother said, "I hardly ever see Veronica Inman around town. She kind of keeps to herself."

Roy ate quickly and excused himself saying he was so tired he could barely keep his eyes open. They finished up the meal.

"You two hurry up and go. Do what you have to do. I'll clear the dishes," said his mom.

It took only a minute for Lila to grab her jacket while he waited for her by the door. They stepped outside into the evening light.

As they climbed into his car, he prayed that talking to Charlie's widow would get them some answers.

For the first time since she'd landed in Montana, Lila was feeling like maybe she would leave here with answers about her father.

Stewart checked his rearview mirror frequently. She understood his vigilance.

"I have a vague memory of Charlie Inman. It seems like he had just moved here shortly before the robbery."

"Yeah, he made his millions in the tech industry and then came out here to buy the old Johnson ranch. Too bad it couldn't stay in the family."

They drove for at least twenty minutes. "How far out of town does she live?"

"We're less than a mile from her property."

The shrill cry of sirens caused Lila to crane her neck. She saw flashing lights. Stewart edged over on the shoulder of the road. Fire trucks, an ambulance and a police car.

"Oh, no." The words seemed to stick in her throat.

Even with the windows rolled up, she smelled smoke before they drove past the sign that said Johnson Ranch.

Flashing lights filled the windshield as Stewart pulled onto the property. The fire trucks were dragging their hoses toward what was obviously the main house.

He patted her shoulder. "You stay here. I'll see what I can find out."

Stewart stepped toward the man who she recognized as his deputy.

A firefighter emerged from the house carrying a woman over his shoulder.

Lila rested her palm on her heart and prayed that Veronica would be okay. Not just for her own sake but because Veronica was a human being who deserved to live.

The firefighter placed the woman on a

waiting stretcher, and the EMTs surrounded her. A moment later, the doors of the ambulance opened and the stretcher disappeared inside.

The firefighters entered the house with their hoses while the ambulance sped away. The yard looked overgrown, and the house appeared run-down.

A little dog burst out of the house and took off running. "Oh, no, he's probably scared to death."

Lila pushed open the door and ran in the direction the dog had gone. She passed through what may have been a garden at some point but now was just tangled, dying plants hanging on trellises.

She didn't see the dog anywhere. "Hey, little guy. It's okay. I won't hurt you." Her eyes scanned everywhere. She bent over, peering under the bushes and dead rose plants. Two bead-like eyes stared back at her. She got down to the dog's level and made soothing sounds.

He whimpered.

She reached out and took him in her arms. He was shaking like a broken washing machine. "So scary. I know."

A sound deeper in the overgrowth caused her head to snap up. She was about to move toward where the noise had come from when Stewart's voice filled the air coming from the opposite direction.

"Lila, where are you going?" He hurried toward her. Fear etched across his features.

"This must be Veronica's dog. He's half-scared to death."

"You should have stayed in the car like I said to." Maybe Stewart was concerned for her safety, but his fear over something happening to her made his comment come across as almost angry.

"I couldn't leave this poor little dog out here." While the dog trembled in her arms, she searched Stewart's eyes. "What's going on? What happened to Mrs. Inman?" Fearful of the answer, her voice faltered.

"The firefighters won't know anything for sure until they get the fire put out and can look around." He turned toward the smoldering house. "They'll probably have to get an arson investigator."

"Was Mrs. Inman able to say anything before the ambulance took her away?" She drew the dog closer to her chest. It was as if his fear matched her own.

Stewart shook his head. "She was unconscious. A neighbor saw the smoke and called 911."

"Is she going to be okay?"

"Smoke inhalation and first-degree burns. They're taking her over to Clemson Medical. They're better equipped than our little ten-bed facility," said Stewart. "I think we should go to the hospital and wait for her to wake up. I told the deputy I would question her in an official capacity. He's going to stay here and have a look around and talk to the neighbor who called the fire in."

"So you don't think this was some sort of accident?" She already knew the answer to the question.

"It just seems a little too coincidental."

When Adam the insurance guy had mentioned Charlie Inman's name, people had been milling around on the street. Anyone could have overheard them.

Stewart rested his hand on her upper back, guided her toward the car, and opened the door for her.

"Let me hold the dog so you can get in. I don't have a carrier. You'll have to keep him on your lap."

Once inside, Stewart handed her the dog. At least the little guy had stopped shaking and was now licking her hand.

As they drove the forty miles to the hospital, the sun had gone down and it grew dark.

The dog, whose tag said his name was Georgie, fell asleep in her arms.

Stewart pulled into the hospital parking lot. "There's a coat in the back seat. We can lay the dog on it. I'll come back and check on him."

He helped her get Georgie settled, and they headed into the hospital. The waiting room was empty. The lady at the administrative desk looked up from the book she was reading when she saw them come in.

"Sheriff Duncan."

"Emma, I need to speak to Mrs. Inman as soon as she wakes up."

Emma was probably ten years older than Lila. Though her hair showed signs of gray, she had a youthful face.

"I can let the doctor know, but it is at his discretion."

"Please tell him it's urgent," said Stewart.

Emma headed down the hallway. Stewart and Lila found a place to sit in the ER waiting area. She sank into the plush chair, grateful it was comfortable.

Flipping idly through a magazine, she didn't even register the words and pictures that flashed across her field of vision. "Mrs. Inman's place looked really run-down. I remember it was quite the showplace when she and her husband first moved here."

"She became kind of a recluse after her husband died. Rumor has it that she's been selling off portions of the land over the years. Probably just the house and a few acres are still hers."

"How did he die?"

"Horse riding accident. Horse bucked him off, and he hit his head."

"Shortly after the robbery?"

"Yeah, maybe a month or so after you left." For the first time, Stewart was able to mention her departure without that note of bitterness, or maybe it was hurt, in his voice.

He pulled his phone out. Though she only heard one side of the conversation, it was clear he was talking to one of his deputies who had searched the site and questioned neighbors. It didn't sound like he had found anything conclusive.

Stewart held his phone close to his mouth. "Well, we won't know anything for sure until the arson guy gets there… Yes, I agree the place was a total firetrap. It could be an accident, a dirty chimney or whatever."

Lila rose to her feet and walked over to a vending machine that held drinks. Nothing looked appetizing.

Stewart said something about getting a city officer outside of Mrs. Inman's room. Stewart must be running with the theory that the fire had been set on purpose and Mrs. Inman's life was still in danger.

Upset by the idea that another person was under threat, Lila paced up the hall and then back down.

When she peeked in the waiting room, Stewart had put his phone away and was massaging his temples and forehead.

"I'm going to go check on that dog."

He burst to his feet. "I'll go with you."

They left the intense light of the hospital for the shrouded darkness of the parking lot. Their footsteps were the only sound as they walked across the concrete parking lot. Stewart leaned close to her as they peered in the back window where the dog was still curled up.

When they pushed through the doors of the hospital entrance, Emma was waiting for them. "Mrs. Inman is awake. The doctor says you can speak to her briefly."

ELEVEN

As Stewart moved down the quiet hallway with Lila, his mind was racing. He understood that the evidence over the fire at Veronica Inman's was still being processed. He was operating on the assumption that it had not been an accident. If Lila's return had brought dark forces out of the woodwork, their decision to question Mrs. Inman had stirred things up even more.

He only hoped they could get to the bottom of who was behind the attacks before more harm came to Lila or Veronica. They stepped into the hospital room where Veronica sat up in bed. She had bandages on one hand and arm. Her eyes were glassy and unfocused, probably indicating she had been given some kind of painkiller.

"Sheriff Duncan." She offered a faint smile and then coughed, drawing her hand to her mouth.

"Can you tell me what happened at your house earlier today with the fire?"

"Not much to tell. I have a wood-burning stove. The house filled with smoke." Clearly upset, she shook her head as her hand fluttered to her neck. "It gets cold at night even in the spring."

"But the burns on your hands and arms?"

She stared at the bandages. "I must have touched the stove or fell against it… I don't know." She shifted in the bed and pulled the covers toward her neck with the hand that didn't have bandaged fingers.

The painkillers were probably heightening her emotional responses. He didn't want to push her too hard, but he needed answers. "Did you see anyone on your property at any time today?"

She let out a heavy breath. "No one comes by much anymore. I'm there by myself, just me and Georgie." Her eyes grew wide as she drew a hand to her mouth. "Georgie…my Georgie."

"The dog is okay." Stewart turned back toward Lila, who stood by the door. "Lila caught him when he ran out of the house."

She stepped close to the bed into the light. "He's a cute little guy."

"Lila? You're Richard Christie's daughter. Why did you come back after all these years?" Her tone held a note of accusation.

Lila looked at Stewart. Her expression held a question. How much was she supposed to share?

"Mrs. Inman, if I could just ask you some questions about what your husband had in that safe-deposit box at the time of the robbery," said Stewart.

Mrs. Inman shifted in the bed then glanced off to the side. "I want to see my dog. I want to see Georgie."

It was clear that asking her additional questions was not a good idea. Lila's presence seemed to have upset her even more.

"I'll see what I can do about the dog." He ushered Lila out of the room. Veronica had been through a traumatic event. Seeing the dog might calm her down. Then maybe she would be able to answer some questions.

Once they were out of the room and a few paces down the hallway, Lila spoke up. "That poor woman. When she moved here, I remember seeing her downtown. She was so beautiful. She was quite a bit younger than her husband. She can't be more than forty now."

Though she still retained some of her former beauty, the years had not been kind to Mrs. Inman.

Lila seemed almost as upset as Veronica. “She sure didn’t like seeing me.”

“Let’s go see if we can talk the powers that be into letting her see her dog. I think that might go a long way to us being able to get some answers.”

Emma was still the only person in the waiting room area. Stewart had a feeling the doctor would nix the idea of bringing a pet into the hospital. “Emma, we need to ask if we can do something on the down-low to help Mrs. Inman.”

“She has a dog she’s really attached to.” Lila stepped closer to him and stared down at Emma.

The receptionist rose to her feet. “Pets are not allowed in the facility. I know the doctor will say no.”

“If we could just bring the dog in for a minute and let her hold it. I think it would go a long way toward her being able to rest and get well.”

The tightness in Emma’s features indicated she could not be swayed.

Lila stepped toward the other woman. “What if Veronica comes to the window in the waiting room, and we can at least hold Georgie up so she can see him?”

Emma took a step back. “That would probably be okay. I have a dog of my own. I know how much emotional support they give."

"We'll go get the dog," said Stewart.

"Wait. I'll need to find out if Mrs. Inman is open to doing that and see if she feels up to getting out of bed."

Emma disappeared down the hallway while they waited. She returned a moment later giving them the okay sign and then grabbing a wheelchair and head ing back down the hallway.

They stepped outside and made their way to the car. Stewart reached to open the back door realizing he'd forgotten to lock it.

"The dog is gone," Lila said.

Stewart flung open the door thinking that Georgie was just on the dark floor of the back seat. He wasn't there either.

A plaintive high-pitched bark came from the edge of the lot where the streetlight didn't reach.

They took off running toward where the noise had come from. There was no way Georgie could have gotten out on his own. Someone must have opened the door and taken him.

They reached the edge of the parking lot, which connected to a lawn with small trees spaced far apart. Beyond that were several houses.

Stewart knew they were walking into a trap. He had not had time to grab his off duty gun.

The dog made yelped as if it someone had stepped on its foot. Stewart's breath caught and he tensed. They had no choice. No way was he going to let that dog be harmed.

"Stay close to me," said Stewart.

He stepped on the lawn and headed toward the source of the yelp. Lila grabbed his hand in the dark and stayed close.

The barking was farther away. Whoever had the dog was running. The first home they came to was surrounded by a high fence with a grove of trees behind it.

Stewart stopped to listen. Lila squeezed his hand.

The silence was disturbing. That dog had to still be alive.

Please, God.

A ballistic barking that cut off suddenly and then resumed like the dog was jerking on his leash and choking himself resonated from deep in the trees. They ran toward the noise, deep into the trees, adjusting their route every time they heard a bark.

As they drew close to the barking, Lila sprinted ahead of him. She was so vulnerable out here, an easy target to shoot at through the darkness. Lila dropped to the ground and gathered the dog into her arms.

She spoke in a soothing tone. “There, there. It’s all right, little guy.”

Stewart pivoted in a half circle scanning the darkness and expecting to be ambushed or shot at. He saw no signs of movement or light in the trees. He stepped in a wider circle, still looking. Nothing.

He returned to where Lila held the dog close to her chest while he whimpered and licked her face. The dog had been tied to a tree with a makeshift leash made of stretchy gauze.

Stewart pulled his pocketknife out and cut the gauze. A realization sunk in that made his heart beat faster. “Lila, we need to get back to the hospital right now.” He held up the gauze. “Our perp must have been in the hospital when he grabbed this.”

She burst to her feet. “He wanted to lure us away so he could get at Mrs. Inman.” They ran back toward the hospital. Lila fell behind as she carried the dog. He waited for her at the door.

They entered the reception area. Emma was nowhere to be found. An empty wheelchair turned on its side rested in the hallway leading to the hospital rooms.

They rushed past a man in a medical smock, coming out of a room.

"Did you see a woman with bandaged hands and maybe a man?"

The man shook his head. "You're talking about Veronica Inman. She should be in her room."

Lila spoke up. "Where's Emma?"

Perplexed, the nurse wrinkled his forehead and took a step back. "She should be at the front desk." He focused on Georgie. "That dog is not supposed to be in this facility. What is going on here?"

"A woman might be in danger. Watch him." Lila placed the dog in the man's arms.

They checked Veronica's room and found it empty. They would have noticed someone being dragged across the patient parking lot or a car speeding away. But the employee parking lot was on the other side of the building. "You stay inside with people where it's safer," said Stewart. "I'll check the back parking lot." It appeared, though, that there were very few people working at this hour.

As he hurried up the hallway toward a side door, he prayed he had not miscalculated the situation and put Lila in danger.

Lila ran down the hallway calling Veronica's name knowing she had to help find the woman. Had Veronica been abducted from the wheelchair? Lila ran back to the reception area.

A flash of color on the far side of the counter caught her eye. Emma lay on the carpet facedown. Lila checked for a pulse. Emma was alive but unconscious.

"Nurse, please. Someone, help me." There had to be some medical staff in this hospital. Where had that guy in the smock gone who they had given the dog to?

She heard tapping sounds and then Georgie appeared at the other end of the counter. The dog sat down and stared at her. A realization sunk in. The man in the medical garb they had encountered was the man who was after Veronica. She scooped up Georgie and ran back toward the room the man had come out of. A nurse came down the hallway, registering surprise at the dog in Lila's arms.

Lila pointed toward reception. "Emma has been hurt. She needs help."

The nurse rushed toward the hospital entrance.

The side door burst open. Stewart was talking on his phone. "Yes, the black truck with the broken headlight. I need a deputy over here ASAP."

Lila entered the room where the man had emerged from when they'd first seen him, terrified of what she might find. Georgie let out a bark.

"Is that my baby?" Veronica's voice sounded weak.

Lila stepped toward the bathroom door. She heard the bolt twist and the door opened. Mrs. Inman reached for Georgie, and tears streamed down her face.

"What happened?"

"A man dressed like a nurse tried to drag me out of the hospital." Veronica spoke while the dog licked her face and trembled with joy. "I got away and locked myself in the bathroom. He must have heard you guys coming."

Stewart stepped into the room. "His truck is still in the parking lot. That means he's on foot. I've got deputies coming to help with the search. They're bringing a boot to disable the truck so the man doesn't try to double back and escape in it. I need to watch the truck and meet Deputy Swain out there." Stewart turned sideways. "All three of us can identify him now."

Once Stewart left the room, Veronica's mood shifted. She glanced nervously at Lila.

"I only saw him for a few seconds," Veronica said. "He wasn't anybody I knew."

Lila had to admit that she was paying more attention to the uniform than the face. She could remember his basic features and build. She hadn't recognized him either.

"Did he say anything to you?"

Veronica drew the dog close to her chest and nuzzled her face in his fur. She was shaking and the tightness in her features communicated that she was upset.

Veronica seemed like a fragile person. They needed her calm if they wanted her to answer their questions.

"Georgie can't stay in the hospital."

"I know."

Lila held out her hands. "I can watch him until you're released. Unless you have someone else in mind." The dog clearly meant a great deal to Veronica. Taking care of him would go a long way toward building some trust.

"No, there is no one to watch him." She placed the dog in Lila's arms. "Thank you."

"I'm sure you'll be out in no time." She rose to her feet as Georgie squirmed. "I'll send the nurse down to help you out."

"I can make it to my room," said Veronica.

"All the same, she probably wants to check you out." Lila hurried down the hall to the reception area.

Emma was up and sitting in a chair, holding an ice pack on the back of her head while the nurse stood over her.

Lila stepped toward her. “Are you okay?”

Emma nodded.

“She’s going to have a bump on her head,” said the nurse.

“I think Mrs. Inman could use some help. She’s headed back to her room.”

“What’s going on here anyway?” said the nurse.

“I’ll have the sheriff explain when he comes in.” Lila wasn’t sure how much information she should even share. “I’ve got to put this dog back in the car. If you could check on Mrs. Inman that would be a help.”

She pushed open the door and stepped out into the cool, dark night. Georgie’s body felt warm pressed against her chest. Her footsteps pounded out an intense rhythm as she headed toward the car.

Shifting Georgie to the side so she could open the door, she placed the little dog on the back seat. A hand went over her mouth, and her arm was yanked behind her and pushed upward to the point of causing pain.

As she tried to wrench free, Georgie barked and then growled.

The man spoke into her ear. “How about you and I go for a short ride?”

He slammed the door to muffle Georgie’s barking. Any time she tried to twist free, he applied pressure to her arm. Georgie bounced up placing his paws on the window, continuing to bark.

Her assailant's hand slipped slightly on her mouth. She took the opportunity to bite his finger, and he cried out in pain and removed his hand.

She screamed. "Help—"

The man pressed his hand back on her mouth, squeezing with such force it hurt. "You shut up."

Trying to wiggle away from him only caused more pain to her face and arm. She lifted her foot and stomped. He yelped and let go of her. She ran three steps before he grabbed her from behind by her shirt. His hand went to her collar, and he yanked her back. She gasped and sputtered for breath.

He let go and pushed her to the ground. She held her hands out to brace for the fall on the concrete. Her attacker's pounding footsteps grew fainter as he neared the edge of the parking lot. When she looked up, two bobbing lights came toward her. No wonder he had run.

Stewart gathered her into his arms.

The deputy put his face close to Lila's. "Which way did he go?"

She pointed in the direction the attacker had fled.

Stewart held her. "It's okay." He stroked her hair. "It's going to be okay."

"Georgie." She could still hear the little dog's muffled yipping.

She opened the back door and petted the upset animal until he calmed down.

With his arm still around her, Stewart ushered her back toward the hospital and pushed the door open. Even though it was empty, the reception area was filled with a warm glow that felt welcoming and safe.

She turned to face him, nuzzling against his chest and weeping. This was all too much to bear. Only the comfort of Stewart's arms buoyed her up.

TWELVE

Stewart wrapped both his arms around Lila and held her close. She was crying so intensely that her body trembled. His heart ached for her. She'd been through a terrifying attack. He'd do anything to take her fear and pain away.

She pulled back and searched his face. "I'm sorry for the waterworks. I'm so overwhelmed."

"I know." He brushed away a tear with his thumb. "He's getting desperate. He knows we've seen him." As she gazed up at Stewart, he was struck by how beautiful she was and how good it felt to hold her even under such trying circumstances.

"It's not just me. Now I've put Veronica's life in danger." The tears started to flow again. "Maybe I should never have come here. I should just accept that I won't ever know the truth about my father."

He held her close and swayed. “Don’t say that. You did the right thing. To want justice and to seek the truth. I’m so sorry I doubted you.”

She pulled away but grabbed his hand, leading him to a sofa. “People could die because of my coming back and poking around.”

They both sat down. “Lila don’t give up now. I’m going to do everything I can to get answers. This case is way more complicated than it looked on the surface.”

As he let go of her hand, he noticed the abrasions and cuts on it. Some pebbles were embedded in her skin. “We should get a nurse to clean that up.”

She stared at her palms as if seeing them for the first time. “I’m just glad my hands took the brunt of the impact when that man pushed me.”

He touched the bottom of her chin so her gaze met his. “We’ll see this thing to the end…together.”

She nodded. “With your help is the only way I could keep fighting. I can’t do this without you, Stewart.” She touched his cheek. Even though tears still glided down her face, she managed a faint smile.

Her touch sent a bolt of heat through him. He jerked to his feet. “Let me see if I can find a nurse." He felt so close to her in that moment that if he didn't leave the room, he would end up kissing her.

That would send such a mixed message. What they had was gone. They were allies now. Two people seeking justice. Two people who still cared about each other. He could at least admit to that.

He rushed down the hallway in search of a nurse. The nurse he'd seen earlier emerged from a side corridor. Her face grew grim when she saw him.

"I sent Emma home. She has been through quite enough tonight." A note of accusation tinged her voice.

"Understandable. There's a woman in the waiting area with some abrasions on her hands. I was wondering if you could have a look at her."

"You do know how to keep me busy." The nurse was trying to sound put off, but he saw kindness in her eyes. "Why don't you have her meet me in exam room one?" She pointed at a door.

"I'll go get her."

Stewart hurried back to reception and gestured toward Lila. "Just this way."

He led her down the hallway, resting his hand on her back.

When they entered the exam room, the nurse was waiting for them. She had already pulled out what she would need and laid it on a tray.

"Hop up here, honey." The nurse patted the exam table.

Lila obliged. "Is it okay if Stewart stays?" When she gazed at him, her expression held a warm quality that drew him in.

"Sure that would be fine," said the nurse.

It was nice that she wanted him to remain close.

The nurse nodded, then opened a packet that contained sterile tweezers. "Now, let me see that hand."

The nurse expertly picked out the pebbles and placed them in a cup she had put on the tray.

Stewart glanced out the door. "How is Mrs. Inman doing?"

"She's sedated." That protective tone the nurse exercised came back into her voice. "She has been through quite enough tonight too. She needs her rest."

"I agree. I have arranged for a city officer to watch her room. He should be here any minute."

The nurse studied him for a long moment and then shook her head. "I'm not even going to ask why." She applied disinfectant to Lila's hands and then put round bandages on the larger cuts.

Lila hopped off the exam table and thanked the nurse.

"I would appreciate it if you would let us know when Mrs. Inman is ready to talk, and if you would pass the message on to the next nurse on duty."

When they left the hospital, the city police officer had just parked his car. Stewart thanked him. "Keep us in the loop if anything happens."

He and Lila walked to his car and got in. Lila looked over the seat at Georgie. Stewart glanced back as well. The dog thudded his tiny tail but otherwise did not stir.

On the drive home, his deputy called.

"Suspect is still at large. We did trace who the truck belongs to, but it looks like it was reported stolen a few days ago."

So two dead ends as far as getting some answers was concerned. "Anything else?"

"Actually, yes, one of the firefighters who was at Mrs. Inman's house called me off the record. Nothing is official until the arson investigation."

"What did they find?"

"Looks like someone plugged up the chimney so the smoke would back up into the house," said the deputy.

Sabotage. A chill ran up Stewart's spine. They needed to question Veronica further.

Stewart was glad Lila had not heard that side of the conversation. He understood all that had chipped away at her resolve. He didn't want to add to her heartache and worry.

As he had thought when he'd originally seen the suspect in the forest, he looked to be about the same age as Stewart and Lila. But he was not anyone either of them recognized, which seemed strange. Trident was not a big town, and the high school had not had that many students. He could arrange to look through the database of known criminals in the area to see if they came up with a match. That might be their next move in bringing the man to justice.

Lila was half-asleep when he pulled up to the ranch house. He squeezed her shoulder. After she got out of the car, she gathered Georgie into her arms, and they made their way up the stairs.

Lila grabbed a dish from the kitchen to give Georgie some water. "Is there anything to feed him?"

"I'll find something for him."

He found some burger for the dog, who ate with great enthusiasm.

After he was done, Lila took Georgie with her and headed upstairs.

After checking to see that all the doors were locked and the windows latched, Stewart went to his room. His east-facing window provided a view of the corral and the road beyond.

It was quiet out there…for now.

He pulled his personal gun out of the nightstand and placed it on top. Though he was beyond tired, he tossed and turned for at least twenty minutes before falling asleep.

He awoke in the night. Not sure what had caused him to stir, he got up and checked both windows in his room. Through the window that gave him a view of the road up the hill, he saw a vehicle rolling by. His hand hovered over the gun until the red taillights disappeared from view.

He lay back down on the bed, though it took some time before he was able to slow his racing thoughts so he could sleep.

He awoke to sunshine sneaking through the blinds. A second later his phone rang. He pressed the connect button and sat up, swinging his legs over thc side of the bed.

"Hello?"

"This is Nurse Amy Fields at Clemson Hospital."

"Yes." Fearing that something had happened to Mrs. Inman in the night, his stomach clenched.

"Mrs. Inman is up and having her breakfast. She will be released after that. She says she's ready to talk, and she is anxious to see her dog."

Stewart rose to his feet. "That's good news. I'll get over there as quickly as I can."

"Actually, she's made reservations at the Huckleberry Bed-and-Breakfast until the smoke damage in her house has been addressed," said the nurse. "She wanted you to meet her there so she can be with her dog."

"Wait. Don't hang up. Please tell her that it is important that she have the officer on duty escort her to where she will be staying."

"I think he may have left…not sure why."

Stewart paced the floor. "Then don't release her until I can get over there."

"She's anxious to leave," said the nurse. "I will do my best to have her stay here, but, really, it's up to her."

Stewart dressed, brushed his teeth and splashed some water on his face.

He hurried downstairs. He was concerned for Mrs. Inman's safety. She didn't have a car. It would be a ten-minute walk from the hospital to the B and B where she would be out in the open.

He found Lila in the living room hand-feeding Georgie morsels of hamburger. Lila was dressed. A cup of coffee sat on the side table by the sofa. “He’s really hungry. We need to get him some food.”

“We gotta go,” he said. “Veronica is being released from the hospital.”

Lila rose to her feet and followed him outside, holding Georgie.

Within seconds, they were both in the car. He shifted into Reverse and headed up the road. He had to do something to ensure Mrs. Inman’s safety. He suspected she held a key piece to the puzzle of what had happened ten years ago.

Lila stroked Georgie’s soft head. His tiny tongue was like velvet when he licked her hand. “I’m going to miss this guy. He’s such a sweetheart.”

Stewart stared through the windshield. His jaw was tight.

“You’re worried about something.”

He let out a breath. “You know me too well. I’m worried about something happening to Mrs. Inman.”

Lila’s throat went dry. “Why? What’s going on?”

“Her protection went off duty, and she’s

probably walking to the B and B where she's staying."

"You're worried that that guy might be watching the hospital and waiting for his chance?"

Georgie whimpered. He was probably picking up on her fear.

He pulled his phone from his pocket. "Find Deputy Swain's phone number. Dial it for me and put it on speaker."

Lila's thoughts raced as she listened to Stewart talk to his deputy about the danger Veronica might be in. The deputy responded that he was closer to Clemson than Stewart and Lila were.

"I'm probably ten minutes away from the hospital," said Deputy Swain. "Hopefully, I can catch up with her."

The rest of the drive went by in a blur. As they passed the Welcome to Clemson sign, Stewart's phone rang. Lila pressed the connect button, and the deputy's voice came across the line.

"It's all good. Mrs. Inman is safely inside the B and B."

Lila let out a breath.

Clemson was bigger than Trident. It was close to a lake and attracted lots of tourists in the summertime. They drove through downtown, which was just coming alive with activity. Lots of art galleries and restaurants and fly-fishing shops.

The Huckleberry Bed-and-Breakfast was on the edge of town surrounded by open fields on two sides. Houses on large lots occupied the area next to the B and B on the west side.

Stewart pulled into the paved driveway.

They got out and entered the reception area where a woman directed them to a back patio. Veronica sat in a lawn chair in the shade staring off into the distance.

Georgie wiggled in Lila's arms. She set the dog down on the tile so he could run into Veronica's arms.

While the dog quivered with excitement, Veronica laughed and spoke soothingly to Georgie.

After a moment she tilted her head. "Thank you for taking care of him."

Lila took a chair close to Veronica. "You're welcome. He's a sweetheart." A phone sat on the table between them.

Veronica touched the phone. "My neighbor brought it for me."

The picture on the phone was of a man on a horse. If memory served, that had to be Charlie Inman. Even after all these years, Veronica kept a picture of him close.

Stewart took a chair as well. His nervous glance at Lila communicated that he wasn't sure how to broach the reason they needed to talk to Veronica, though she seemed to be in better spirits than last night.

He wasn't a man who openly expressed everything that he was thinking. Years ago, when they had been in love, she had gotten good at reading what was going on with him. The skill was coming back to her, maybe because some tentative connection was forming between them that had once been broken.

Lila knew from experience how traumatic events like what Mrs. Inman had just been through made it hard to deal with intense questions. But they needed information, and they needed it quickly.

They talked some more about Georgie and how nice the B and B was. Mrs. Inman relaxed a little. The lady who ran the inn brought out some lemonade for everyone. Lila sipped her drink.

She petted her dog. "I know there was a policeman outside my room last night. What's going on? Am I still in danger?"

Stewart cleared his throat. "We think that what happened at your house was not an accident."

Veronica's face paled, and she shook her

head. "I gathered that what happened with that man in the hospital wasn't some random thing either. Why would anyone want to hurt me?"

The widow was so isolated that whatever gossip had swirled through Trident had not reached her. But she'd had a strong reaction to Lila the night before, probably connecting Lila to her father and the robbery.

"We need to talk to you about the safe-deposit box your husband had at the bank where my father was the manager." Lila spoke as gently as she could.

Veronica's eyes grew wide. Georgie jumped out of her lap and began to sniff around. "That was so long ago. That bank robbery." She rubbed her arm in an agitated way.

"It was ten years ago. But it seems that Lila coming back to find out what really happened has upset someone involved to the point of violence. We think there was someone else involved in that robbery who doesn't want the truth to come out."

Veronica combed her fingers through her hair in a jerking motion, clearly upset. "You think my husband had something to do with it?"

Lila was struck by the conclusion Veronica jumped to. "We weren't thinking that at all.

I understand your husband died shortly after the robbery."

Veronica clutched her shirt at the collar with her unbandaged hand. "He was thrown from a horse and hit his head. I don't understand where this is going."

Mrs. Inman's agitation visibly increased. She wiggled in her seat as her gaze darted around.

"Was he with anyone at the time of the accident?" Stewart asked.

"No, he was out riding by himself."

Maybe Stewart had intended to distract from direct questions about the robbery to calm Mrs. Inman down.

She got up and gathered her dog into her arms. She tilted her head toward the sky and let out a breath.

"Veronica, the only reason we wanted to talk to you was because we know that your husband's safe-deposit box was one of the ones targeted. We understand he filed a claim. What was in that box that was so valuable?"

"Jewelry. Some very expensive pieces that Charlie had given me and some family heirlooms." She rested a hand on her dog's belly. A tear rolled down her cheek.

Lila and Stewart remained silent.

"After my husband died, I found out that he

had lied about our finances. He had overextended himself. He had a great deal of debt, bad investments, gambling, expensive toys." She lifted her glass and took a sip of lemonade. "Do you know what it's like to realize your whole life is a lie, the embarrassment of it?"

Now Lila understood Veronica's reason for living such an isolated life. She reached out and patted the other woman's hand.

"The sad thing is, I think he thought if he didn't keep up appearances of being the richest man in town that I would leave him," said Veronica. "I know he was older than me by fifteen years, but I loved him." She swiped a tear away from her eye. "Sorry, I know that's not what you came here to talk about."

"It appears that of the three boxes targeted for the robbery, your husband was the only one who filed an insurance claim," Stewart said. "So what was in those other boxes wasn't worth filing a claim over, so why bother to drill them at all?"

Veronica looked at Lila then at Stewart. Light came into her eyes and her expression communicated a realization. She sat Georgie on the ground and walked over to the edge of the patio staring out at the open field and the trees beyond.

"Mrs. Inman?"

She whirled back around. "It didn't make sense to me at the time. After Charlie died, I found one of the pieces of jewelry that I'm sure was on the insurance claim. A gold broach with emeralds that had been his mother's."

"Maybe he was mistaken about what was in the safe-deposit box when he filed the claim and he found the broach later."

She shook her head. "It's just now making sense to me...the paperwork I came across. I think he held on to that broach for sentimental reasons. I don't think any jewels were in that safe-deposit box."

"What makes you conclude that?"

"I should have paid more attention to what was going on financially when he was alive. After the insurance claim came through, he was able to pay down some debt. But the amount was almost double of what the claim was for."

"So you think he filed a false claim and then sold the jewelry that he said was stolen?"

She nodded. "He was trying to get us out of trouble without me finding out."

Veronica came back to her chair and sat down. Georgie sat at her feet.

"If there was no jewelry in that box, what

was in there that was worth killing my father over?" Stewart shook his head.

"I have no idea," said Veronica.

No one spoke for a few seconds. Stewart rose from his chair. "I think we should get going. Thank you for your help."

"Sure." Mrs. Inman got a faraway look in her eyes as she held her dog.

"Mrs. Inman," said Stewart, "I'm going to make some arrangements for an officer to check on you. It would be good if you didn't leave the B and B."

"I'm fine with that. Now that I have Georgie. My house won't be livable for a few days, if not longer," said Veronica. "I have a lot to process. I feel like I didn't even know my husband."

As they walked through the reception area of the bed-and-breakfast, Lila felt as if the world had been turned upside down with what they had learned.

THIRTEEN

Stewart made arrangements for an officer to check on Mrs. Inman as they walked to the car.

His mind whirled with what Veronica had concluded. There was no way to prove it at this point.

They got into the car. He rested his hands on the steering wheel.

Lila faced him. “Kind of a bombshell, huh?”

He nodded and then turned the key in the ignition. “I’m not sure what to think. There had to be something in that safe-deposit box. Maybe Charlie Inman was somehow involved. This wasn’t a straight-forward robbery but some kind of insurance fraud.”

Lila clicked into her seatbelt. “I feel sorry for Mrs. Inman. I think she loved her husband.”

He pulled out onto the street.

As he drove, Stewart tried to bring his fuzzy thoughts into focus. "I think the next step is to figure out who that guy was at the hospital. He might be able to get us some answers. If we turn what we know over to the FBI, maybe they'll reopen the case."

He drove to the sheriff's office. "We can access a database of criminals in the area. With the basic description of his features we give, the computer will sort out any that clearly don't fit."

She touched her stomach. "Can we get something to eat? I only had half a cup of coffee before we left the ranch house."

"Sure, there's a bakery across the street from the sheriff's office. I can grab something for both of us while you start looking through the database."

He pulled into the parking lot by the sheriff's office and opened the door. Both deputies must be out on calls. He directed Lila to a room with a computer. They sat beside each other as he opened up the program and typed in the data that would establish the parameters of the search.

His fingers tapped the keyboard. "We know the suspect was white, male and…did you notice eye color?"

Lila shook her head. "There was nothing

distinctive about him. Brown hair. His eyes might have been brown too. Certainly not striking in any way. I would say he was over six feet."

"We'll set the parameters at five-ten and above. Brown hair, but it could have been dyed." The description was generic at best. The man had had no scars, acne or visible tattoos.

The computer indicated it was sorting and then the first photo came up on the screen. Both of them shook their heads. He showed her how to bring up the next photo. "When you get to one that is a maybe, you can just put it in this folder here so you can look at it again. The gut reaction, though, is usually the one you go with when you first see the photo. Don't overthink it."

"Got it," she said. "You saw him too. Are you going to look through these?"

"Yes, but it's best of we do it separately, so we don't influence each other. Memory is a tricky thing. We saw him for all of ten seconds. If we both come up with a match in our folders, that's a strong indicator that he might be our guy."

She clicked on two more photos. "This will take a while, won't it?"

"Yes, for sure. Most police work is tedious

like that." He pushed back his chair and stood up. "I'm going to get us something to eat."

He hurried across the street to get coffee and breakfast sandwiches. While he waited in line for his turn to order, he realized he had left Lila alone. With him taking time off, the deputies were probably both out on calls. The sheriff's office could not be locked in case someone needed assistance.

When he glanced over his shoulder through the window, the only car in the lot was the one he drove. The line seemed to be moving incredibly slowly. Once he got his food. He rushed back across the street and entered the sheriff's office.

When he peeked in the room with the computer, Lila was not in there. His heart beat faster as he set the food down. He called her name, rushing through the office down the hall. He peeked into the jail area and called her name again.

"I'm here." Her voice came from the main area of the office.

He ran back up the hallway. "Lila, where did you go?"

"My eyes were blurry from looking at the screen. I stepped out to get some fresh air. I was just on the side of the building."

He ran to her and clamped his hands on her arms. "Don't do that again."

"I'm sorry. I wasn't thinking."

"I was worried about you." He gathered her into his arms and held her close. "We still have to be on our guard."

"Even at the police station?"

"Yes, always." He pulled back and gazed down at her. "Don't know what I would do if something happened to you."

Her lips parted. He saw affection in her eyes. "I appreciate that, Stewart, I do."

The intensity of her gaze caused him to let go of her arms and take a step back. Kissing her would only complicate their lives.

She stared at the floor. "Guess I should get back to looking at those photos." Her voice had switched to a neutral tone.

They both knew better than to pursue the feelings that had risen to the surface. "I gotta make some phone calls," he said.

He listened to Lila's footsteps as she patted down the hallway before sitting at his desk and looking up the number for his contact at the FBI.

While he sat listening to the phone ring, she returned and placed his coffee and breakfast sandwich on his desk. She disappeared down the hall again.

The contact did not pick up. Stewart left a message summarizing what Mrs. Inman had said and asking if he could see the files about who the other two safe-deposit boxes belonged to and if the owners had been interviewed.

He hung up the phone. He found himself thinking about Lila again. He took several sips of coffee and then picked up his sandwich and walked to the room where she was.

"How's it going?"

"I put a few possibilities in the folder. But nothing jumps out at me. Who would have thought that there were so many criminals in this county?" She brushed a strand of hair behind her ear.

The radio in the office squawked. He ran to pick it up.

Deputy Swain identified himself. "We may have a lead on your guy."

"Go ahead."

"The truck was reported stolen by an older gentleman, Nathan Wheaton, just outside of Clemson. He thinks that a fellow who did some landscaping work for him might have taken it."

"Do you have a name?"

"Travis Kindred. He was paid cash so there was no W-2 filled out or anything. We're trying to track down an address for him and find out if anyone in town knows him."

"Let me know what develops. I'll see what I can pull up on him."

Stewart headed back down the hallway to where Lila was. She scooted over so he could access the keyboard. He typed in the name. Nothing came up.

Stewart thought for a moment, then kept typing. "Let's widen our search to neighboring counties."

A photograph came up on the screen.

Lila leaned back in her chair. "That's the guy."

The dead eyes of the man who looked back at her on the screen gave Lila the chills. The birth date listed indicated he was a couple years older than her. "He's not anyone I've seen before. He would have been, like, twenty at the time of the robbery."

Stewart scrolled down on the screen. "Looks like most of his convictions are drug related." He kept reading. "Some of these convictions are for other parts of the Northwest. He must move around a lot."

Lila sat back in her chair. "Do you suppose he lived here ten years ago and then came back when he saw the story about the getaway car?"

"Maybe. We can find out if he has family in the area." said Stewart. "Something feels off kilter to me though. Travis wasn't someone we knew in high school." He thought for a moment. "Let's go talk to Nathan Wheaton the guy who employed Travis. Maybe Travis talked about his background."

They got in the sheriff's vehicle and started to drive.

The radio squawked.

Deputy Swain's voice came through. "A man who matches Travis Kindred's description is holed up at a Rest Easy motel by the interstate between Clemson and Trident, room twelve. Deputy Ridge and I are en route in separate vehicles."

"I'm on my way." Stewart pressed the accelerator. "I don't have time to drop you off or go back to the police station. You will need to stay in the car."

Stewart zigzagged through the city streets. Once they were out on the highway, he increased his speed, weaving in and out of traffic. Within five minutes, Deputy Swain radioed that he was in place and watching the motel where they believed Travis was.

They passed the billboard that advertised

the motel at the next exit. Deputy Ridge's voice came across the radio.

"I'm in place at the turnout just off the exit."

Stewart pushed the talk button on the radio. "Gotcha. Our ETA is about three minutes."

The motel was next to a truck stop. Stewart pulled into the parking lot. They passed Deputy Swain's car positioned by the motel office and entrance to the parking lot.

"I have visual on room twelve." Stewart spoke into the radio.

"Roger. How do you want us to proceed?" said Deputy Swain.

"Did you talk to the front desk person? Does she or he know if Travis has a car?"

"He didn't list a license plate number when he checked in."

"Doesn't mean he hasn't acquired a car since then," said Stewart.

The curtain on room twelve moved. Stewart sat up straight. The radio was still in his hand. "I think he's aware we're here. Let's move in." His voice intensified. Each word was like a pounding drumbeat.

Lila's heart beat a little faster. Tension permeated the air around her.

Stewart pushed open the door. "Stay low. I don't want him to see you in this car. Lock the doors."

With her eyes just above the dashboard, Lila watched as Stewart drew his weapon. Deputy Swain ran toward room twelve. When he got within a few yards, he took his gun out as well.

She watched as the deputy stood off to one side of the door, gun held close to his body. Stewart knocked on the door, shouted something and then positioned himself clear of the door.

Movement on the far side of the motel caught her eye.

A man wearing a baseball hat and oversize coat had come around the corner. Though he attempted to look casual by strolling with his hands in his pockets, the glancing side to side suggested a level of panic.

He pulled a gun and aimed it toward Stewart, whose back was turned to him.

Every muscle tensed in Lila's body as the world seem to move in slow motion. She reached for the window button as the man raised the gun and stalked toward Stewart.

When she yelled Stewart's name the word seemed to evaporate bcfore it left her mouth.

Stewart looked toward her, then pivoted with his gun raised to the man. The man shot once. Stewart returned fire.

The shooter drew his attention to the car

where Lila was. She slid down lower in the seat. He slipped behind another car for cover. Though he was out of view from Stewart and Deputy Swain, Lila could see him. The deputy took cover behind a maid's cart, pushing the cart toward where the suspect was crouched.

Stewart yelled something as he aimed his gun at the car where the suspect was. Stewart slipped behind a different car, and his head bobbed up by the trunk area.

The perp stayed low and ran to another car that was on the edge of the lot.

She had a clear view of what was happening while Stewart and the deputy did not. She had to do something. She reached for the radio. It took her a second to find the talk button.

"Stewart, he moved to the tan car at the edge of the lot."

"Roger that." Stewart spoke from his shoulder radio.

Her attention had been on the radio. When she looked up through the windshield, the suspect was coming straight toward her with his gun aimed.

FOURTEEN

Stewart watched in horror as the man fired his gun. The bullet glanced off the body of the sheriff's car.

The suspect continued to advance.

Stewart rose and ran across the parking lot.

"Put the gun down."

The suspect dashed toward Stewart's SUV, disappearing on the driver's side. Stewart felt like he'd been punched in the gut. Lila was in there.

A shot was fired.

The driver's side window shattered.

Stewart sprinted the remaining distance to where the suspect had lifted his gun and was going to shoot again into the car.

Protocol dictated that he give the man every chance to surrender.

"Put the gun down." Though inwardly he was scared to death for Lila's safety, his voice remained strong and authoritative. He put his finger on the trigger. Stewart fired a shot.

The man glared at Stewart and then took off running.

Deputy Swain saw what was happening and sprinted to the edge of the parking lot where the suspect had disappeared behind some bushes that grew along a secondary road.

Stewart ran the remaining distance to the car and peered through the broken window. Lila was crouched on the floor of the passenger side. Her hands rested on the back of her head.

Fear gripped his heart. "Lila?" His throat was so dry he could barely utter her name.

She glanced up, staring at him with glazed eyes. Her face was drained of color. "I'm not hit."

Deputy Swain's voice vibrated through the radio. "Suspect has gotten into a blue compact car and is headed east on Old Mill Road."

Deputy Ridge, parked by the interstate exit, came on the line. "Roger that. I am in pursuit."

They had counted on the suspect heading toward the interstate. There would be a delay in how quickly his deputy could get rerouted. Deputy Swain was on foot but probably returning to his car to give chase.

Stewart flung open the door and swiped the glass off his seat with his arm. He got behind the wheel. He could get to Old Mill Road faster than his deputies.

Stewart grabbed his radio and notified the other two lawmen that he was after the suspect while he started the SUV.

Lila pulled herself up and put her seatbelt on. "I'm sorry I drew attention to myself. But he was going to shoot you."

"You did what you had to do." He hated that she had been put in danger. Just as he had concluded before, there was no place for her where the culprit would not come after her. He still believed the safest place was with him. "I'm grateful you saved my life."

If Lila hadn't been with him, he might be dead.

He accelerated when he turned out of the lot onto the frontage road that led to Old Mill Road. Deputy Swain emerged from a cluster of trees running full out to get back to his car.

Stewart took a corner at a high speed then turned onto the dirt road where the suspect had gotten into a car. There were two houses, a trailer and some outbuildings, all with cars by them. That must be where the perp had stolen the car.

Deputy Ridge who had been positioned by

the interstate exit came through the radio. "I'm going to see if I can cut him off at the crossroads. Looks like it's about a mile from the turnoff onto Old Mill Road."

"Roger that. I don't have any visual on the suspect yet." The engine revved as Stewart pressed the gas pedal. A dust cloud indicated a car had just been there. They were closing in.

The speedometer clicked up past fifty. A dangerous speed on a dirt road. He rounded a curve and saw the taillights of the other car.

"I have visual on the suspect," said Stewart.

"Roger that. I'm in place," said Deputy Ridge.

Stewart drew closer to the suspect's car. The road straightened, and he could see his Deputy Ridge's car up ahead at the crossroads. He assumed the deputy had taken cover behind the car and was ready to shoot if required.

When it drew close to the deputy's car, the suspect's car veered off the road, lumbering across of field. Stewart turned off as well. Lila clutched the armrest, bracing herself for the bumpy ride. As the terrain became more uneven, the suspect's car rolled to a stop. The driver's side door burst open. The perp emerged and ran toward a cluster of trees.

Stewart got out and pursued the man on foot. His gun was drawn as he entered the forest. He listened for any indication of which way the suspect had gone while he scanned for any movement that would give the man away.

His deputy's voice came through the radio. "Deputy Swain just arrived. He's flanking this cluster of trees on foot. If the suspect is in there, we should be able to cut him off."

Fear over Lila being put in danger permeated his thoughts. "Deputy Ridge, please stay close to Lila."

"Roger that."

Stewart advanced in the most likely direction the suspect would have gone. His eyes scanned every tree and space in between.

Shouting and then gunfire came from deeper in the grove. Stewart pivoted in the direction of the noise. The suspect barreled toward him clutching his shoulder.

Stewart raised his gun. "Stop, police."

The suspect collapsed on the ground. Stewart ran toward him. The man gritted his teeth as a bloodstain spread across his shoulder and then he passed out.

Stewart radioed dispatch for an ambulance.

Deputy Swain emerged from the trees. His

gaze moved to the unconscious man on the ground.

"I had no choice but to shoot him," said Deputy Swain.

"It's all right," said Stewart. The suspect's chest rose and fell with his breath. "The bullet probably tore through muscle. We'll get him treated for a gunshot wound, and then maybe we can get some answers."

"I can follow the ambulance back to hospital. I'll stand guard and notify you when he's ready to talk," said Deputy Swain.

Stewart waited with his deputy. Within minutes, they heard the shrill cry of the ambulance. The unconscious man was loaded on a stretcher. Stewart returned to where Lila still sat in the sheriff's car.

Her expression held a question mark.

He flung open the door. "We have him in custody. He needs medical attention. Soon as he recovers, we'll conduct an interview."

The paramedic emerged from the trees hauling the stretcher.

"So that's it. It's over." She stared through the window as the man they'd been chasing was loaded into the ambulance.

Stewart nodded. He got into the car. The doors to the ambulance were closed, and the paramedics jumped in the cab. As the ambulance pulled out, Deputy Swain returned to his vehicle and followed.

"Everything feels a little surreal to me right now," said Lila. "I guess I'm relieved."

"Me too." Stewart turned the key in the ignition, and the car rolled forward. Deputy Ridge pulled out behind him.

"This means I can go back to my folks' place and finish sorting through stuff."

What she said took him by surprise. "That's what you want to do?"

"I came back here for answers about what happened to my father. I'm hours away from being able to close this chapter of my life. I think I held on to that house because it was my link to the past."

"So you're going to sell it?"

She nodded. "Once we find out how Travis connects to what happened ten years ago and find out what he knows about my father, there is nothing to keep me here."

At a loss for words, Stewart turned onto the secondary road that connected to the interstate.

For the remainder of the ride back to Trident, he and Lila talked about shallow things that didn't matter. His thoughts operated at a low-level hum. The case would soon be closed. Lila was leaving. He entered the town limits and drove to Lila's house.

She offered him a faint smile. "As soon as you know anything, you'll tell me, right?"

"Sure. I imagine he'll be in surgery for a bit and then it will take some time for him to be coherent enough to answer questions."

"Once everything is wrapped up, I'd like to come out and say goodbye to your mom. I'm glad we got to know each other again."

"Sure, no problem," he said.

She pushed open the door but turned back to face him. "Thank you for everything, Stewart. I couldn't have done this without you."

His throat grew tight as he tipped his hat to her. He waited, watching her walk up the street to her house as a deep emptiness invaded his heart. He was happy for her. Once they got answers from Travis, she would have accomplished what she set out to do. Still he couldn't let go of the sadness at the thought of her leaving. Selling the house probably meant she didn't see herself returning.

He drove away, wishing that things between them could have ended differently.

Lila unlocked the door to the home where her life had fallen apart and stepped inside.

Her footsteps echoed on the floor as she moved to retrieve the keys to the garage and some trash bags.

She let out a heavy breath. Probably before the week was over, she would be headed back to Seattle and the life she'd built there. Stewart was not the boy she'd left behind. He was a man who had grown into maturity and had become someone worth admiring once he was no longer in his father's dark shadow.

Though she sensed there was still that spark of attraction between them, they were both different people than they had been at eighteen. When she stepped outside, it had just begun to rain. Hurrying toward the garage, she shielded her head with her hand. She unlocked the garage and stared at the shelves that held memories of the person she used to be and of her mother and father.

When she'd decided to rent the house out, she'd asked the property manager to simply remove anything from the house that appeared to be personal. She pulled the box nearest the door off a shelf and opened it up. The picture of her and Stewart at the prom was on the top of a pile of framed photographs.

She lifted the photograph and studied it. Her eyes glazed with tears. For her and Stewart, theirs was a story of innocence lost by the choices of other people.

Some things were just not repairable.

She worked for hours sorting into keep, donate and throwaway piles. When she looked up through the dusty window of the garage, it was dark. She'd been working in dimming light this whole time. She tried the light switch but the single bulb hanging from a wire didn't work. No surprise there. She found a camping lantern. The lighter in the camping supplies still had some spark. She hung the lantern from a hook in the middle of the garage.

The rain was still coming down when she returned to the house to get something quick to eat so she could return to work. The sooner she finished this task, the faster she could put the house on the market and let go of her last tie to Trident and all the dreams she'd had at eighteen. When she reached the house, she was soaking wet. The wind beat against the panes of glass.

She stepped inside, retrieved a clean bathrobe that was part of the service the property manager provided and tossed her wet clothes into the dryer. The kitchen was stocked with nonperishables and canned goods. She got herself a glass of water and put some peanut butter on crackers.

She checked her phone. No call from Stewart yet.

Finishing her crackers, she wiped the crumbs off the counter.

An abrupt banging noise caused her stomach to tighten. She stepped through the silent, dark rooms trying to figure out the source of the sound, which was coming from the back of the house.

Lila hurried through the laundry room where the dryer was still whirring. The back door was slamming against the frame in the wind created by the storm. She closed the door and pushed the handle to lock it. She had looked out at thc backyard when she'd thrown her clothes in the dryer. The door must not have been fully latched when she closed it.

The trees in the backyard bent and shook in the wind. Shadows danced across the yard.

Lila waited until her clothes were dry. Using a garbage sack to shield her from the rain, she returned to the garage. She went inside and stared at the bags she'd already filled.

Her parents' furniture had been stacked in a far corner of the garage. This was the stuff that the property manager had deemed not suitable for the vacation rental. Her father's desk, her mother's sewing machine cabinet and beat-up wooden kitchen chairs precariously stacked. Other trunks, boxes and totes made up the remainder of the Jenga pile.

A creaking sound caused her to take a step back as the chairs came toward her. She put her hand up to shield her face. An object hit her in the head, and she twisted around and crumpled to the ground on her stomach. A heavy object landed across her back. She was pinned from the shoulders down, unable to move. More weight was put on top of her.

She heard footsteps but could not lift her head high enough to see who it was. Someone was moving things around. She struggled to get free of the trunk that had landed on her. One of the full garbage bags blocked her view. She could hear the person shuffling and moving the bags to create a wall. A door slammed. More banging noises. The sound of glass breaking and then the space grew darker. The camping lantern had been thrown or knocked on the floor.

She screamed. "Help, someone, please help me."

The wind and rain rattled the single window in the garage. Then she detected another noise, a sort of whooshing crackle. But it wasn't until she smelled smoke that she realized the lantern had been used to set a fire.

Lila could only move one arm a few inches. The other arm was pinned from the elbow down. There was nothing within her grasp that she might be able to use to escape. She'd left her phone on the counter in the kitchen.

Whoever had been in here intended for her death to look like an accident.

The man lying in the hospital bed with a bullet wound was not who they thought he was.

She coughed as the smoke grew thicker and darkness enveloped her.

FIFTEEN

The whole time he did ranch chores, Stewart had been anticipating the call from Deputy Swain, but it did not come until after dark.

"Yes," said Stewart.

"We got a problem," the deputy responded.

His stomach tightened. "Something's happened to Travis?"

"He was breathing when I left my post to go to the bathroom. I was gone less than five minutes."

"The wound wasn't that bad." Stewart leaned against a fence post. "What happened?"

"Medical staff are trying to figure it out. The coroner is on his way," said the deputy. "Sir, I don't think he died of natural causes. What are the chances of him stopping breathing in the brief time that I'm not at my post?"

"You think someone slipped in there." Stewart stalked toward his truck.

"I do. I'm going to start questioning the staff to see if they saw anyone."

"Keep me posted. I gotta call Lila. This means she is still in danger, and Travis was probably just hired muscle who knew too much." Stewart swung open the door to the truck he'd borrowed from his brother as he ended the call. He pressed in Lila's number. It rang four times and went to voice mail.

He shifted into Reverse and headed toward town, trying to quell the dark thoughts that invaded his awareness. He didn't know anything yet.

The drive through town seemed to take forever.

He pressed the gas pedal to the floor. Lila's house was on a large lot on the edge of town down a dirt driveway.

He arrived at her house, jumped out of the car and ran up the stairs to her house. The door was unlocked. He stepped inside calling her name. Her phone sat on the kitchen counter.

His heart was racing by the time he made it to the back of the house where he had view of the garage. She must still be out there sorting through things. He hurried down the back stairs and ran toward the garage. As he drew near, he smelled smoke. The only window was cloudy with it.

When he tried the door, it didn't budge. He slammed his whole body against it. This time it moved a few inches like a weight was pressed against it. Thick smoke rolled out and he stepped back coughing. The smoke had been contained within the garage. The nearest neighbor may not have seen the fire to call it in. The rain from earlier must have soaked things enough so it didn't spread to the outside of the building.

He dialed 911 and reported the fire.

But he couldn't wait for the fire department.

Remembering there was a spigot and a hose on the side of the house, he ran to turn the water on, then grabbed the hose and hurried back toward where the smoke still billowed out. Using his shirt to filter some of the smoke he put his weight against the door so it moved even more. Then he sprayed into the open doorway until it cleared enough for him to see. It looked like someone had stacked garbage bags against the door. The fire itself was contained by the garage door. Still using the hose, he stepped inside, hoping to clear more of the smoke.

Calling Lila's name several times, his heart

squeezed tight when his cry was met with only silence.

She can't be dead. Dear God, let her be okay.

The hose would reach only a few feet into the garage. Though heat from the flames was intense, it was the smoke that was more of an obstruction.

He sprayed in a wide arc hoping to be able to see into the depths of the garage. Then he heard coughing.

His spirits lifted. He dropped the hose, covered his mouth with his shirt collar and moved toward the sound.

He found Lila on the floor, facedown and buried beneath a trunk and some garbage bags. He lifted the bags, coughing so bad that he bent over. Nearly collapsing from smoke inhalation, he got down on his knees and pushed to get the trunk off her.

With the smoke and the lack of light, he couldn't see much. He gathered her into his arms and stumbled toward the door. Twice he had to lean against shelving to keep from giving in to the weakness that inhaling so much smoke caused.

He stepped through the open door. Still holding Lila in his arms, he fell on his knees and drew her close, kissing her forehead and thanking God that she had not succumbed to the smoke.

In the distance, he heard the sirens as the fire truck approached.

This fight was not over yet. Whatever had happened ten years ago was still worth killing the one person who had always cared about finding the truth.

The firefighters, ambulance and city officers all arrived at the same time. Lila remained unconscious as she was loaded into the ambulance.

"I want to go with her," said Stewart.

While they got Lila set up in the ambulance, one of the paramedics gave Stewart a quick look-over and offered him an oxygen mask. Stewart slipped in beside Lila. Her face was turned toward him. He brushed her hair off her cheek.

How could he let this happen? At the back of his mind, he had thought that it didn't make sense that a man their age with no connection to them had been involved in the robbery. Travis must have been hired by someone to stop Lila from digging for the truth by killing her. His drug history and his transient lifestyle made him a great candidate for such an ugly job.

They arrived at the hospital. The paramedics whisked Lila into the facility through the ER, handing her off to the waiting physician after reciting her condition and the circumstances that had led to it.

Stewart walked up to the front desk to talk to the receptionist. "The second there is a change in her condition, I want to know, for better or worse."

Maybe it was that she knew he was the sheriff even out of uniform or the way he spoke with such authority, but the lady behind the desk didn't argue with him or ask if he was a family member.

"Will do, Sheriff."

Deputy Ridge came up the hallway. They were in the same hospital where Travis had died only hours before.

"Any news?"

"The coroner thinks there was foul play. Everything is still speculation at this point, but the petechial hemorrhaging suggests strangulation."

Stewart opened his mouth to respond but ended up coughing.

A look of concern crossed the deputy's face. "Don't you think you should be checked out, sir?"

"I'll be all right. Minor smoke inhalation. Lila got the worst of it. I don't know how long she was passed out inhaling that stuff before I found her."

"A bit of good news before all this went down. Your contact at the FBI phoned the office, said with what you uncovered concerning Mrs. Inman, they are going to reopen the case and work it from a different angle."

"I suppose that's good news." The man behind this had to know that he would be caught eventually. Stewart patted his deputy's shoulder. "You've put in a long shift. Why don't you go home and rest?"

Deputy Ridge nodded and headed through the lobby toward the exit.

Feeling exhausted, Stewart found a comfortable chair in the lobby. He closed his eyes but remained awake, his thoughts bouncing around from worry over Lila to what the events of the night meant. Travis must have been killed because he knew who had hired him and would talk.

A hand rested on his shoulder. He opened his eyes to see the doctor who had taken over Lila's care. "She's in a room now, resting."

"How bad is it?"

"She suffered from smoke inhalation."

Stewart rose to his feet. "I want to be in the room with her even if she isn't awake."

The doctor ushered Stewart down a hallway to a dim room where Lila slept in the hospital bed. Stewart found a chair, intending to stand guard over Lila.

If the man behind all this had killed Travis in this hospital, there would be nothing to stop him from going after Lila here as well.

Lila awoke in a dark room. Light streamed in from the hallway. The sound of soft snoring caught her attention. Stewart sat in a chair, head tilted to one side, arms crossed.

Her spirits sank. In the hospital again. She was achy, and her chest hurt every time she took in a breath. Coughing made the pain even worse. A sense of despair invaded her thoughts as she recalled what had happened. Travis could not have been well enough to leave the hospital. Someone else was involved.

Staring at the ceiling as the tears streamed down her cheeks, she felt like this nightmare would never be over. How many more times would the man behind this come after her? Next time, he would succeed. At this point, even returning to Seattle might not stop the attempts on her life. They'd uncovered so much already. The attacks felt more like revenge for her snooping around in the first place, done by someone with deep anger and bitterness.

The nurse came in to check her vitals. Stewart stirred awake. Once the nurse left the room, he cleared his throat. "I have some bad news. Travis died. It looks like foul play."

Lila was so numb she couldn't think of what to say. She sat up with much effort. The tears flowed again, this time more intensely.

Stewart gathered her into his arms. He smelled like smoke as her cheek brushed the soft cotton fabric of his shirt. He rubbed her back and swayed until she stopped crying.

His hand glided over her hair. "I know this is a lot to deal with."

"It feels like too much right now, Stewart," she said. "I want to give up. But I don't think this man, whoever he is, will stop even if I go back to Seattle. It's like he's driven not only to keep us from finding out what really happened with that robbery but for shear vengeance. If I die, the FBI might be able to find him. It feels personal."

He pulled away and sat back down in the chair. "The FBI has reopened the case based on these attacks and Mrs. Inman's theory about her husband."

"That's good news."

Stewart didn't answer right away. He must be trying to think through all that had happened.

She reached for the call button. "You know, I'm kind of hungry. Do you suppose they have anything to eat at this hour?"

A few seconds after she pressed the button, a nurse popped her head in.

"Could I have something to eat and maybe some ginger ale to settle my stomach?"

"The cafeteria is closed at this hour, but I can rustle you up a snack." The nurse looked at Stewart. "How about you, sir?"

"I could use some hot tea with lemon and honey." He touched his neck. His throat probably felt as scratched as hers.

"Give me a moment," said the nurse. "I'll be right back."

Lila listened to the woman's soft-soled shoes pad down the hall.

"I'm glad you're here with me, Stewart," she said. She felt safe in his arms, but there was some deeper connection there that she had to admit to when she looked into his eyes.

Stewart glanced away and then stared at the floor. "I was worried that he might try to come after you while you were here since he got to Travis that way."

The feelings she was having were brand-new—different than they had been ten years ago. What she felt for him now wasn't some soft-focus romantic idea born out of naivete. It was something much deeper. Maybe selling the house and leaving so quickly was too dramatic a step.

But Stewart's response indicated that he was acting out of a sense of duty. The feelings probably didn't go both ways. Yet she thought she had sensed something shift between them.

The nurse returned with a tray that held some prepackaged cookies, a ginger ale and a steaming mug.

Stewart thanked her, grabbed the tea and sat back down.

Lila sipped the ginger ale. "You want one of these packets of cookies? Fig Newtons always were your favorite, right?"

After sitting the tea on the windowsill, he leaned forward to grab the packet she held out to him. "Yes, they are. Some things never change."

"But some things do change…like us."

"Sure, we grew up." He tore open the cookies and took a bite.

"In a way, we both kind of got stuck. Neither one of us has moved on and met someone else. Did you ever ask yourself why?"

"I never got over the way you hurt me, Lila.

I didn't want to go through that again." His voice took on a hard edge.

His words stabbed her heart. He had built a wall around himself that she could not scale, and to a degree, she was responsible for it. "To be honest, when I first left town I thought that I'd always come back here someday. I think that's why I held on to the house. I kept telling myself that I just needed time away to work through stuff. One year turned into two and then I got so busy with work…it was easier to stay away than to try to come back and fix what I had broken."

"Thanks for admitting that. It means a lot to me." His voice was no longer harsh. "I get that you lost your dad and your mom in less than a year. Maybe you were just trying to outrun the pain."

"That was part of it I'm sure," she said.

It was the first time since her return that they were able to talk about what had happened without growing upset.

She relished the sweetness of the moment. That they could talk this way made her feel closer to him.

In an instant, the warm glow she saw on Stewart's face hardened as he turned his head sideways.

A second later, the glass in the window

Stewart was sitting by shattered. His mug smashed to the floor.

Stewart leaped to his feet, scooped her up out of the bed and fell to the floor. Another shot reverberated around the room. Both of them crawled toward the hallway on their bellies.

A nurse appeared in the doorway. "What's going on here?" Her expression changed when she saw pieces of glass all over the floor.

"Get down," Stewart yelled.

The nurse stepped back and then ran down the hall. The chaos of excited voices could be heard outside the room.

Weakened from all her body had been through, Lila struggled to get to safety. The third shot hit something metal in the room.

Risking his own life, Stewart stood up and dragged Lila through the door to the hallway. Still in pain, she pushed herself up and propped herself against the wall.

A female voice came over the intercom. "Code silver. Active shooter. Please shelter in place."

"Stay here." Stewart cupped her shoulder.

Before she even had time to respond, he had turned and was running for the side exit. The one closest to where the shooter had to have been positioned. She could hear him talking on his phone calling for backup.

If the deputies were at the office, it would take at least five minutes for them to get here. Longer if they were out on a call.

That meant Stewart would be going after the shooter alone, and he was not armed.

SIXTEEN

Stewart ran around the hospital to the approximate place he believed the shooter to be. The man must have figured out which room they were in. It was only a ten-bed facility. Trident Hospital was a single-floor critical-access hospital, not equipped to deal with complex medical situations. The shooter could have peered through windows until he saw Lila and Stewart. Or maybe he wandered the hallway to find them and then took a position outside to make a quick escape.

The shots had sounded like they'd come from a pistol not a rifle. That meant the shooter had taken aim at close range. Stewart could not wait for backup. By then the culprit would be long gone.

He sprinted across the lawn to the shattered hospital window. There was a small park with boulders, a fountain and a copse of trees where a man could shield himself from view and have a direct line of fire into the room where Lila had been.

Bracing for an ambush or bullet, Stewart stepped toward the first boulder. The fountain hummed and bubbled as he walked past it. The space was empty.

His heart pounded as he listened for any sign of someone close by.

When he rounded the second boulder, he saw shell casings on the ground but nothing else. The guy had fled. Houses with fenced yards were all there was beyond the park.

Stewart had gotten here fast enough that he would have seen or heard a car on the street start up. The culprit must still be on foot.

A barking dog several houses down caused Stewart to burst into a run.

His phone rang, and Deputy Swain spoke. "In the hospital parking lot. Deputy Ridge has gone into the facility to stand guard and take statements."

Stewart spoke between breaths as he kept running. "I'm en route up the ally by First Street. I think the perp is still on foot."

"Roger that. Will come around with the vehicle to patrol the streets. He's got to come out somewhere."

Stewart ran toward where he'd heard the barking dog. When he approached the house, the German shepherd inside the fence let him know he was on duty pacing and watching Stewart.

Surveying the area, he tried to guess at where the man could have gone. He saw the marker for a trailhead. Most of the neighborhoods in Trident had walking trails around them. That was his best guess at where the culprit might flee.

The trees grew thicker as he got close to the start of the trail. He ran over a wooden bridge that opened into a grassy meadow that the trail wound through.

The sound of a car starting up told him that he was probably too late. He hurried toward the noise, hoping to get a look at the car hidden by a cluster of trees. He came out onto the street where the shooter must have driven away on.

There were no houses out here, only an open field. The shooter had planned his exit well. The whole thing had taken a degree of calculation. The man who set the fire was probably the same man who shot at Lila in the hospital room.

He must have been watching Lila's house to see that she had survived the fire. Discouraged, Stewart notified his deputy of the possible route the suspect would have taken.

Deputy Swain's voice came through the phone. "Did you get a make on the vehicle?"

"Negative," said Stewart.

With a heavy heart, Stewart returned to the hospital. Even though he knew once the man was caught, Lila would leave town, he wanted this to be over for her. He hoped she would find the answers she was looking for and that her life would no longer be under threat.

The sheriff's SUV as well as the city police car were in the hospital parking lot when he returned. He stepped inside. About six of the medical staff were gathered in the lobby with the police officers. There was a patient in a wheelchair as well, but he didn't see Lila anywhere.

He spotted the nurse who had brought them food coming up the hallway and ran toward her. "Where's Lila?"

"There's a lounge off the main hallway with no windows. She wanted to wait there for you."

He found Lila flipping through a magazine in the lounge. She gazed up at him when he entered the room.

"I don't have to ask. I can tell by the look on your face. He's still out there, isn't he?"

"It's that obvious, huh?" When they had been in love, she'd often known what he was feeling even before he spoke. To know someone inside out like that revealed a deep connection. Now it seemed she had regained the skill in reading his mood when he walked into a room. Perhaps it meant they'd formed a new connection. He moved to take a seat beside her. "I'm so sorry. I want this to end for you." He placed his hand over hers.

She didn't pull away from his touch. "I don't know if this will ever be over. Maybe I should have just stayed away." She sighed. "The doctor said I can be released. If the crime scene people are done, I'd like to go by my place to see the damage."

"Sure, we can do that," he said.

When they walked through the lobby, the crowd of people had mostly broken up. Deputy Swain came toward him.

"I took everyone's statement," he said.

"Did anyone see a stranger in the hospital at any time or someone acting suspicious?"

The deputy shook his head. "They are down to a skeleton crew as it is. There's only one other patient besides Lila."

The small hospital had no security. It would have been easy enough to slip in and out unnoticed. They might have security cameras at the entrances and exits.

He thanked his deputy and walked toward

the exit with Lila. They drove through silent dark streets to her house.

Before the car had even come to a full stop, Lila pushed open the door and ran toward the garage.

He turned off the car and followed behind her. By the time he got to the garage, she had pushed open the door and stepped inside. He came up behind her and used the flashlight on his phone to illuminate the space.

They coughed at the acrid stench of smoke, charred wood and the chemical smell of burnt plastic.

"All those memories." Her voice faltered. "My past is being burned up, like I wasn't even here."

He turned to face her in the dark. "I'm sure some of it can be salvaged." The pain he heard in her voice made his chest tight.

"Can you shine the light on the side where there wasn't any fire? I want to take a box or two back to your place and sort through it. I don't want to stop this process."

"Sure," he said.

As Lila moved deeper into the garage, her coughing intensified. She picked up a box, and they stepped outside into the fresh air. She put the it on the ground.

"I just did more damage by coming back to

Trident. I put Mrs. Inman in danger. I stirred up trouble when everyone else was happy to let it go."

"No, Lila, don't say that," he said. "You were right. I was wrong. You deserve to find out what happened to your father."

She fell into his arms, trembling from crying. She tilted her head. "It's like being trapped in a nightmare."

Her face was so close to his, he could feel her breath on his skin when she spoke. "I get that. None of the official investigations brought anything to the surface. Only your determination has done that."

Silence fell between them. More than anything he wanted to comfort her, to quell the anguish she was going through. He leaned toward her. His lips found hers. He kissed her gently at first. Memories of what they had been to each other stirred, and he deepened the kiss.

When he pulled back, she still rested her hand on his chest. His arms remained wrapped around her waist and back.

"Wow, what was that about?"

A hundred explanations tumbled through his head. Had their love for each other been renewed? Or maybe he had never stopped loving her. The pain of her rejection had masked those deep feelings. He didn't know. The cavalcade of emotions raging inside his heart were hard to sort through. He knew he needed to say the thing that would release her to go back to the life she had built in Seattle. "Guess it was just for old times' sake."

"Yes." Her voice had taken on a neutral tone. "For old times' sake and the memories."

"It's been a long day. Let's go to the ranch house," he said.

They got into the car and drove through Trident, where most of the downtown windows were dark. By the time they reached the city limits, they'd encountered only two other cars. As he drove on the country road, he checked the rearview mirror. If they had been followed or someone was going to try to run them off the road, he had to be ready.

Lila sat in the passenger seat and stared out at the night. An uncomfortable silence fell between them. What had that kiss meant anyway?

Her heart beat faster when she thought about it. She had not expected such an intense stir of emotions. Was it really just about who they had been to each other all those years ago?

Or had a brand-new connection grown between them? It was clear from Stewart's explanation that he saw the kiss as being about the past. She had been vulnerable and in need of comfort. If he wasn't going to read more into it, then she probably shouldn't either.

They arrived at a quiet, dark house. He carried the box of memorabilia in for her, and they stood in the living room.

"I'm still a little stirred up from all that's happened. Think I might make myself a cup of chamomile tea." Really, it was the kiss that was making her mind race.

"Do what you've got to do." Stewart didn't seem to want to make eye contact.

Okay, so the kiss had been an impulsive mistake, and now they were both in an awkward place.

She entered the kitchen and put the kettle on to boil. A yard light illuminated the ranch hand's house. The lights were off, and his car was parked outside. The backyard and the corrals behind the house were all dark.

Stewart poked his head in just as the kettle whistled. "Make sure the kitchen door is locked."

"I will." She poured the steaming water into a cup and then swished the tea bag back and forth. Even the act of making the tea was calming. She took her first sip of the warm liquid.

She heard Stewart's voice in the next room as he talked on the phone. The conversation sounded intense.

Holding her warm mug, she stood on the threshold between the kitchen and living room just as he finished the conversation and turned to face her.

"That's my neighbor up the hill. He spotted lights down by the old homestead a while ago. I've got to go check it out. Lock the door behind me. I have my key. Mom's probably asleep."

She nodded.

He hurried across the wood floor and flung the door open. She heard his car start up as she moved toward the door to lock it.

She took her tea upstairs to the bedroom where she was staying. Her window provided a limited view of the road Stewart was on to get to the old homestead. She caught sight of his red taillights for only a moment.

Lila took her mug downstairs then changed for bed. She had just thrown back the covers when she heard noises downstairs, footsteps. Her first thought was that Cindy was up and walking around, but wouldn't she be barefoot or in slippers at this hour? The sound was more like someone in boots trying to be quiet. Maybe Stewart had already come back.

Stewart's brother had a key, but why would he be showing up at this hour?

She hurried out into the hallway. The downstairs was completely dark.

"Stewart? Cindy?"

Her hand reached for the stair light. A repetitive banging noise reached her ears. Her heart beat faster. That was not the noise she'd heard earlier.

She rushed down to the living room. The noise was coming from the other side of the house where Stewart's office was.

Grabbing a poker from the fireplace, she walked toward the noise and peered inside Stewart's office. A latch on a window had come loose and the window was flapping in the wind. She stepped across the floor. After propping the poker against the wall, she reached out to pull the window back toward the frame and secure it.

Her attention was drawn to the photos Stewart had on a shelf. One was the prom photo she also had a copy of. All the other photos looked more recent.

"Lila?"

Stewart's voice made her jump.

She touched her palm to her heart. "Sorry, you scared me."

"What are you doing up in this part of the

house?" His gaze focused on the fireplace poker and then back at her.

"I heard noises like someone walking around with boots on." She pointed at the window. "This window was open and banging against the frame."

He stepped into the room and grabbed the poker. "Was this a precaution?" His shoulder brushed against hers as he straightened up.

His proximity made her heart flutter and brought back the memory of the kiss.

Stewart's mom stood in the doorway. "What's going on?" Cindy was barefoot and wearing a bathrobe. "I thought I heard someone call my name."

"I heard noises. Sorry to wake you." She didn't want to worry Cindy. "It was probably nothing."

"If you're sure." Cindy studied both of them.

"I've got this Mom," said Stewart. "You get some sleep."

The worried look remained on Cindy's face as she turned and padded down the hallway.

Lila waited until Cindy was out of earshot. "Stewart, I think someone was in the house. It sounded like a person with boots on was walking around."

"Are you sure that wasn't the window banging?"

Now she wasn't so sure. She shook her head. "Maybe."

"We can't take any chances," he said. "I'll have a look around inside and outside. Why don't you try to get some sleep?"

"What happened at the old homestead?"

"I didn't see anyone. It was hard to tell in the dark, but it looks like some things have been moved around. I'm going out there in the morning to have a look in daylight."

"I guess I'll go back to bed." She wanted to ask him why he'd kept the prom photo on display but thought better of it. They were finally in a place where the hostility over the past had subsided. She wanted to leave town on good terms.

Lila moved through the dark living room and up the stairs to her room. She slipped beneath the soft covers and closed her eyes. Downstairs, she could hear Stewart going from room to room, probably checking that doors were locked and windows latched.

Though he had seemed dismissive of her theory that someone had been in the house, it was clear from his actions that he was not taking any chances.

SEVENTEEN

The morning sun woke Stewart, though the fog of sleep lingered. He'd had a restless night sleeping a couple of hours at a time and then rising to check that the house was secure and that his mother and Lila were okay. It was disconcerting to think that someone could have been in the house. He wondered if the lights his neighbor had seen by the old homestead had been someone approaching the house on foot going through the old homestead to the ranch house. Though he hadn't found any sign of a forced break-in, the culprit could have come and gone by that window. The latch was in need of repair, and maybe it had provided a point of entry. Stewart might have been lured to the old homestead, so Lila was more vulnerable in the ranch house.

Still, there had been no attack. Going into the house was a bold move. Maybe the person feared getting caught and had changed his mind.

He rose and showered. By the time he entered the kitchen he could smell fresh coffee. The kitchen was empty. When he peered out the window, he saw Lila and his mom talking in the garden. He had a fleeting thought that maybe Lila would return to Trident for visits in the future. Maybe she was closing a chapter by finally making the decision to sell the house, but it seemed like she was rebuilding the relationship with his mother. He and Lila had come to a place of healing and connection.

Why had such an idea entered his mind anyway?

He took a sip of the rich, warm brew and watched as Lila and his mother gathered a bouquet of spring flowers. The two women were laughing and talking in an animated way.

The truth was the notion of Lila not being in his life at all made his chest feel hollow. Had they worked through the past enough to at least have a friendship? Or, if once they had answers about her father, would she just be gone forever?

Lila saw him through the window and waved. She spoke to his mother and then headed toward the kitchen door. She entered holding a handful of flowers. "Your mother said there was a mason jar I could use as a vase."

He opened up the cupboard and retrieved one for her. She filled the glass with water and set it on the table. "So pretty. I wish I had time to paint them." A look of serenity permeated her features as she arranged the flowers. "What do you have in mind for today?"

"I need to go to work in the afternoon. My deputies have been a bit overworked. This morning I thought I would head over to the old homestead to see what I can find. You're welcome to come with me."

"Sure, I'd like that. Could I go into town to see what I can salvage from that garage?"

"I can give you a ride, but you can't be there alone. Maybe I can get Roy or my brother to be with you and give you a ride back to the ranch house."

He finished his coffee, and they headed out to the old homestead. He parked the car and walked to where the foundation was. "Last night in the dark, it looked to me like things had been moved around, but I couldn't see well enough to be sure. I can't explain it. It just felt like something had been disturbed."

They walked around the area. Lila worked her way toward what had been the backyard where there was a well, a rusty tractor and a shed that leaned to one side. She stopped. "Stewart, didn't there used to be some logs here or something heavy?"

He moved to where she was pointing. The flattened ground, exposed roots and bugs all indicated that an object had recently been taken.

"Why would someone want to take rotting logs?"

A deeper search indicated that other objects had been moved as well. Stewart couldn't recall exactly what kind of debris was around the homestead, just pieces of metal and equipment, parts of old furniture. He found places where the brush and grass had been flattened as if something had been dragged over it.

Lila found an empty can of sweet tea that looked like it had been a recent addition to the area. "Someone was here not too long ago. I wonder why."

"Me too," he said.

His thoughts turned to the cattle rustlers. The homestead provided a partial view of the cattle that were in the pasture closest to the ranch house but not the best view. Besides, all the cattle that had been reported stolen were in remote pastures where a trailer could be brought in in the dead of night and go unnoticed.

Someone who had intended to get at Lila while she was in the ranch house would not have lingered to drink a tea or move things around.

He wanted to believe that what had happened here was completely disconnected from the attacks on Lila, but he had the feeling that was a false hope. The thought of someone wandering around on his property for any reason was disconcerting.

When they stepped away from the shelter of the overgrown trees, aware of how exposed they were, Stewart grabbed Lila's hand. "Let's hurry back to the car."

Their vehicle was parked out in the open. He stared up at the hill, a perfect place for someone to hide with a rifle and take aim.

Lila got into the passenger seat and drew her seat belt across her lap. "I keep waiting for the next attack too."

"Sorry I was being so obvious," said Stewart.

"If word gets out that the FBI has reopened the case, do you think that would make him leave town?"

Stewart shrugged. "I don't know what

to think. I just know we can't let our guard down."

They returned to the ranch house and ate a hearty breakfast. Stewart advised Lila to stay inside while he got some chores done before heading to work.

Though there was plenty to be done farther from the ranch house, he opted to deal with repairs and feeding that provided him a view of the road leading to the house. Stewart loaded up bales of hay and drove to where the cattle were in the field close to the house.

By putting the truck in neutral at a gradual incline, it would roll slowly while he tossed the bales for the cattle. Once the grass greened up, he would no longer have to supplement with hay.

He stopped the truck and stared down at the field where his cattle grazed, the homestead nearly concealed by overgrown trees, the ranch house, Roy's trailer and the road leading to the house. He called his brother to see if he would be available to stay with Lila while she gathered more boxes and give her a ride back to the ranch house. His brother agreed to help.

"I'll send you a text when we're on our way into town."

"Sounds good," said Elliot.

After doing chores around the barn and fixing a tractor, Stewart stepped into the ranch house. His mother's classical music wafted down the hallway. He didn't see Lila anywhere, but she had sorted the box of memorabilia that she'd brought with her into two piles on the coffee table. The bathroom garbage can was in the living room filled with papers and some photographs.

He trotted upstairs. Lila's bedroom door was open, and he could hear her talking on the phone.

"So you think we should just hold on to the furniture for staging the house and then sell it?"

She was taking the next step to put the house on the market. Why did that bother him so much?

He popped his head in, and she looked up, murmuring into the phone, "Sorry, can you hold a moment?"

"I just need to get into my uniform, and then we can head into town. My brother can come by and help you out at your house and give you a ride back here."

Lila nodded and then returned to her phone call.

She was waiting for him in the living room when he came out dressed in his uniform.

His brother was at Lila's house when Stewart pulled up to drop her off.

While Lila walked toward the garage, Stewart approached his brother. "Don't let her out of your sight."

"I've heard some of what has been going on. I'll watch her closely," said Elliot.

Stewart got into his vehicle and headed up the street. When he glanced in the side-view mirror, he could see his brother taking the box that Lila handed him while they stood outside the garage.

Stewart's radio crackled. Deputy Ridge's voice came on the line. "Sir, thought you'd like to know we caught our cattle rustlers in the a.m. hours."

"Where at?"

"Over in some fields that Grayson leases north of Trident," said the deputy.

That was miles from the Duncan ranch. "Is it a sure thing?"

"Pretty cut and dried. We caught them loading the cattle, and they confessed. Two guys with previous records for theft."

"Doesn't get any easier than that," said Stewart. "Wish every case wrapped itself up in a pretty package with a bow like that."

"I getcha. No breaks yet with the attacks on Lila?"

"No. Has the crime scene report come back from Travis's death?"

"Not yet. The only good news is that the FBI wants to send an agent up here."

Though the crimes were linked, the agent would be focused on what had happened ten years ago because bank robbery was a federal crime.

Stewart drove through the city streets to the sheriff's office. He parked his car and stared through the windshield, not really seeing the building in front of him. Would the arrival of the FBI agent be enough to scare the culprit away?

He doubted it. To his way of thinking, the only thing that would guarantee Lila's safety would be to catch the man behind the attacks.

Though the perp hadn't come after Lila for a while, Stewart had a feeling that what they were experiencing was the calm before the storm.

Lila loaded the last box into Elliot's truck. "If you don't mind, I need to go inside and make some decisions about the furniture in the house."

"Sure, I'll come with you," said Elliot.

She appreciated that Elliot was taking his

protection duty so seriously. Stewart must have had a word with him.

She gazed around the living room. Some of the furniture had belonged to her parents, and some had been purchased by the property manager. She wouldn't keep everything that belonged to her mom and dad, just a few pieces for sentimental reasons.

"This place looks way different than when I used to come by here after school and hang out with you and Stewart."

"Yes, it has kind of lost that lived-in, warm feel. Now it just gives off that pristine hotel vibe," said Lila. Some of the paintings her mother had done still hung on the wall. Lila would take those with her. For all her struggles, her mother had nurtured Lila's artistic ability and taught her much of what she knew.

Elliot walked around the living room and then directed his attention down the hallway. "I remember you guys would play badminton with me in the backyard."

"I never minded that you were a bit of a tagalong."

"Thanks for saying that. I was kind of the annoying little brother." He took his hat off and twirled it in his hands. "The truth was it just felt good to be in the glow of the two of you being so in love and so right for each other."

"That was a long time ago," she said.

"I know that what you had together changed because of the robbery. I get that we can't undo the past. All I'm saying is that from a twelve-year-old boy's perspective, I don't ever remember seeing two people who were more in love and more right for each other than you two were back then."

"Some things just can't be restored," she said. "Stewart and I are not the people we were ten years ago."

Elliot nodded in response. "Stewart was pretty torn up after you left."

"Hurting him was not my intention when I drove out of town. I'm deeply sorry about that. I think at some gut level I knew that the only way I could find some clarity was to separate myself from this place. I just need a minute more to look at what is here and make some decisions."

"I'll be waiting for you in the truck."

She wandered around the house, taking note of the furniture she wanted to keep. In her mind, the voices from the past, conversations she'd had with her father, played on a loop. It had been her father who had sat at the table with her helping her with algebra. The depression and the medication often meant her mother slept or simply couldn't focus.

Lila could not reconcile that picture, a man who was kind and patient, with a man who would steal and kill another man, even if that man had been an angry, unfair cheat.

Lila removed one of the paintings from the wall and stepped outside where Elliot sat behind the wheel waiting for her.

He leaned forward to fire up the truck. She placed the painting in the back seat and got into the passenger side of the cab. They drove through town past the sheriff's office. Stewart's work vehicle was not parked outside. He must be out on a call.

Elliot dropped her off at the ranch house and helped her carry the boxes in. The music floating up the hallway told her that Cindy was working in her studio.

Lila had sorted through two boxes when she thought to ask Cindy if she would like to join her for a cold drink.

She wandered down the hallway and knocked on the half-open door. She called Cindy's name, shouting to be heard above the music. She pushed the door open. Cindy was not in the studio. Yet the music was still playing as though she had stepped out for a minute, intending to return to her work. Cindy's phone rested on a table by the door. Lila turned off the music. Her heart beat a little faster as the quiet sank in.

She checked the powder room. Cindy's car was still parked outside. She hadn't gone anywhere.

Lila moved from one downstairs window to another not seeing any sign of the other woman. She ran upstairs to where the windows would provide more of a view of all sides of the property. She had a direct view down into the garden and the barn that was close to the house.

Remembering what Stewart had said about not going outside, she retrieved her phone and called his number. His phone went to voice mail.

"Stewart, I'm a little concerned. It looks like your mom just left her studio and wandered off."

Lila paced the floor and then checked all the windows again. She understood how the creative mind worked. It was possible that Cindy had just needed to think about her project and had gone for a walk without the distraction of a phone. But would she have left the music playing like that?

Taking her phone with her and hoping Stewart would call back, she moved toward the front door. A can of orange soda sat on the entryway table. Lila lifted it to see that it was full, as if Cindy had put it down along with her phone, intending to come back. Had the other woman seen something out the window that had alarmed her? Lila stepped out onto the porch. A horse wandered by not too far from the house. The animal lowered her head and chomped on some grass.

"How did you get out?" As though her chest were in a tightening vise, the breath left her lungs, but her inhale was shallow. Stewart had suspected sabotage the last time the horses had gotten out.

Stepping back toward the door, she tried Stewart's number. Voice mail. Again. "Stewart, it's me. Something isn't right. At least one of the horses is out again, and I still can't find your mother."

She was about to return to the house when she heard muffled pounding and the faint sound of a voice in distress. Lila stepped off the porch and ran toward the noise. It was coming from the barn where Stewart kept his tools and the horse tack.

Lila ran faster, and the shouting grew more intense.

She recognized the voice as Cindy's.

"Help, someone, please help me."

Lila ran up to the barn. A tractor blocked most of the door. “Cindy, it’s me.”

“Oh, thank you. I can’t get the door open. I’ve been out here forever.”

“There’s a tractor in the way,” said Lila.

“The door must also be barred. I couldn’t even get it to budge.”

Lila leaned over the tractor to see what Cindy meant. The door was locked from the outside by placing a flat piece of wood through two L-shaped pieces of metal.

“I don’t know how to operate the tractor, and I can’t reach the bar until it’s out of the way.”

“We have to move the tractor. The door opens outward. Is there a key in it?”

“No.”

“The extra ones are in here. Which tractor is it?”

Lila read the brand name pasted on the side of the tractor.

“I’ll shove the key underneath the door. It’s on a string. Give me a second.”

Lila glanced around the farm, seeing only the horse.

“I have it.” The thick door muffled Cindy’s voice.

Lila dropped to the ground and peered past the beefy tractor tires. “Did you leave the house because you saw that horse was out?”

There was about half an inch of space between the bottom of the door and the barn floor. The key appeared, and Lila reached for it.

"Yes, I came in here to grab the tack to get that horse. When I went to open the door, it had been secured." Even through the thickness of the wooden door, Cindy's sounded distraught and afraid. "Then I heard that tractor."

It was clear that Cindy had been the victim of sabotage, but she had not been in any danger before. Even though Lila knew it was dangerous to be out in the open like this, she couldn't leave the other woman here until help came. Maybe whoever had let the horse out had intended for Lila to be the one to come outside to put him back.

When that didn't work, the culprit had changed tactic and locked up Cindy.

Lila rose to her feet and took in the surroundings, remembering that her attacker had shot at her from far away with a rifle. Her gaze darted everywhere. There were a dozen places someone could set up a rifle and take aim.

Her hand was shaking as she placed the key in the ignition. "We'll have you out of here in just a second."

Lila had never driven a tractor before. It

looked like there was a gearshift. She reached to push it into neutral. Her phone buzzed, and she stopped to look. Stewart. She pressed the talk button. Stewart spoke first.

"Lila, what's going on?"

She smelled an odd smell. An object hit her head, and she crumpled to the ground.

Right before her world went black, she could hear Cindy's frantic voice. "Lila, are you okay?"

EIGHTEEN

Feeling a sense of foreboding, Stewart drove past the barn toward the ranch house. He took in the scene. The tractor was parked too close to the barn, and the barn door was flung wide open. Houdini grazed in the front yard.

Lila had left cryptic messages, and when he called her back, she'd been cut off. He could hear what sounded like a woman shouting in the background.

He stopped the car in the middle of the road and ran toward the barn. No one was inside. He called Lila's name and then ran around to where the other horses and the pig were still secure in their respective pens.

He raced for the back of the house into the kitchen. When he flung open the door. His mother and Roy were sitting at the kitchen table. His mother was sipping something hot in a mug. Lila sat on a kitchen chair that was pushed away from the table. She had a blanket around her. She stared at the floor with an unfocused daze.

"Lila, I got your message. What happened?"

"She's all right. Someone locked me in the barn and then knocked Lila out when she came to help me."

Roy spoke up. "He ran off when he saw me coming."

"Which way did he go?"

"Up toward the road. He must have had a car parked there back in the trees," said Roy.

"How long ago was that?"

"Ten minutes. I had to move the tractor to get Mrs. D out. Then Mrs. D stayed with Lila until she came to. I ran up the road a piece but didn't see anyone or a car."

The guy was probably long gone by now.

"Did you get a look at him?"

"He had a baseball hat on," said Roy. "My focus was on Lila lying on the ground and Mrs. D. crying out. He was slim and in pretty good shape."

Stewart cupped his hand on Lila's shoulder. "You okay?"

She looked up at him as her gaze cleared. "I lost consciousness, but I think I'm okay."

He knelt down beside her. "I got here as fast as I could."

"It's not your fault. I know you told me not to leave the house, but I heard your mother crying out."

"The ladies were pretty shook up. I made Mrs. D some tea," said Roy. "Got Lila some water."

"We should get you to the doctor to be checked out."

"I'm tired of doctors." A note of weariness entered Lila's voice. "I don't feel dizzy or anything. I think I'd be better off just taking a nap."

Roy rose to his feet. "If you don't mind, I have to get going. Still got to unload that hay before dark, and I've got some welding to do."

"Sure. Thanks, Roy, for all your help," he said.

The ranch hand exited through the back door.

"I'll stay with you if you like," said Stewart. "Maybe I can call off my shift."

"You don't have to do that. We'll stay inside until you get home."

Cindy rose to her feet, holding the mug of tea. "I'm going back to the studio. That was enough excitement for a lifetime."

Stewart scooted a chair beside Lila's and draped his arm on the back of hers "Are you sure you're okay?"

"No, I'm not okay, but I don't want you to miss more work because of me." She drew the blanket tighter around herself. "That is the closest he's gotten to me. What if Roy hadn't shown up when he did?"

Stewart took Lila in a sideways hug, and she rested her head against his shoulder. He waited until she pulled away.

"Thank you, Stewart. I feel better."

He didn't. He feared the man would come back. "You remember how to shoot a gun, don't you?"

"I haven't fired one in years, not since you and I used to practice together."

Stewart stood up and paced through the living room to his office, where he retrieved a revolver from the drawer. When he returned Lila had moved to the living room and had placed another box on the coffee table. There were two full trash bags as well as piles of papers, photos and photo albums, and some sketches and unframed paintings.

"Mom still practices enough to be proficient with this." He placed the gun on the side table by the sofa. "I've only got a few hours left on my shift, and then I'll be home. It sounds like Roy will be out in the shop if you have any trouble."

She rose to face him. The look on her face

was one of utter defeat. "What if this never ends? What if this man is never caught?"

The culprit was relentless. At this point, the attempts on Lila's life seemed more vengeful than preventing her from finding out the truth. Lila had theorized that he might just follow her to Seattle. The FBI reopening the case was not public knowledge yet, but maybe the suspect sensed that he was running out of time.

Stewart took her into an embrace and held her close. "We're going to catch him. One way or another." He found himself not wanting to leave her. "I don't feel right about going. I'm going to stay with you."

She rested her head against his chest.

It felt so right to have her in his arms.

His radio squawked, and the deputy came on the line. "Got a domestic over on 212 Evergreen Lane. Could use your help. Neighbor called in, said he could hear yelling and threats."

"You need to go," she said. "You can't strand your deputy in a difficult situation."

He didn't know who lived at the address. He spoke into his radio. "On my way." He kissed her forehead. "You know the drill. Lock the doors behind me. I'm going to see if Elliot can come by."

She followed him to the door. Before he

stepped off the porch, he heard the deadbolt slide into place.

Stewart got into his police car and turned up the road heading into town. His GPS told him that Evergreen Lane was in a part of town where newer homes were being built. He was five minutes away from the location when his deputy spoke through the radio.

"We got a problem."

"Go ahead." Tension coiled around Stewart's torso.

"The house on 212 Evergreen Lane is a foundation with framing. It's not occupied. The houses on each side of it are under construction as well. There is no one home at the nearest completed house."

"False alarm." Stewart spun around in the road. His first thought was that he had been lured away from the ranch house. "I need to go back home."

His car sputtered and then stopped altogether. He stared down at the empty gas gauge. The tank had been filled only a few days ago. Now he knew that he had been set up.

"You need to come pick me up now," said Stewart. "Lila is in danger."

"On my way," said the deputy.

Stewart pushed open the door and stepped out onto the street. Within minutes, he saw

Deputy Swain's car turn onto the street and head toward him.

He barely came to a stop as Stewart flung open the passenger's side door and jumped in. The breakdown had cost him precious time.

He prayed they weren't too late.

Cindy's music spilled out of the studio while Lila sat down to continue sorting through the items that chronicled three lives. She lifted a pile of larger photos, most of them eight-by-tens, and started sifting through them.

She tossed the first three. Her gaze rested on a picture of her father with some of his friends at an Elk's Lodge meeting. Her father had hated those meetings but had felt an obligation to show up because he was a bank manager. She moved to throw it away, but then looked at it closer. She recognized Stewart's dad and Roy. But it hadn't clicked with her who the fourth man was. She'd glanced only briefly at the picture of Charlie Inman when it had been wallpaper on Mrs. Inman's phone. Four men, two dead, one disappeared and only one left alive.

A familiar voice pelted her back. "Look what the smart girl found."

Lila whirled around to face Roy. He pointed a gun at her. He was wearing gloves.

She was two steps away from the revolver that Stewart had left for her. Too risky.

"Cindy," she yelled.

He took a step toward Lila. "Trust me, she's not going to hear you. She's out cold with what I put in her tea." He reached past her and picked up the revolver. "This might come in handy." He shoved it in his pocket. Why would he need two weapons?

He waved the gun. "I suggest you come with me right now."

Lila planted her feet. "Why?"

"Because revenge is a dish best served cold, and you are dessert." He gestured with the gun. "Through the kitchen."

She took a step forward, and he moved to one side so he could follow her. She was trying to piece together what had happened ten years ago. Charlie must have enlisted Roy to steal the jewels, telling him he would get them and Charlie would file an insurance claim.

"The jewels in the safe-deposit box were not real, were they? Charlie kept the real ones to sell and collected on the insurance."

He pressed the gun into her back. "Hurry up."

"Charlie betrayed you, so you saw to it that he died on that horse."

She crossed the threshold into the kitchen.

Roy stood close enough to her that she could smell that faint scent of alcohol and sweat. The same smell she had detected right before she was knocked out. She reached for the unlocked door. When Roy had heard Stewart's voice on the phone, he must have realized he'd be caught so he had made up the story about the man attacking her.

Roy put the key back on the hook by the door. He'd apparently lifted it at some point. Maybe he had been in the house that night and realized he'd be caught if he came after her then. She swung the door open. There were scratches all around the lock, so it would look like there had been a break-in.

A car that was not Roy's was parked on the lawn close to the back door. She saw now what the plan was and why he hadn't shot her in the house. He was setting things up so he couldn't be linked to the crime. "You're not even going to leave after you kill me, are you?"

"Now that would look suspicious, wouldn't it?" he said. He shoved her toward the car. "You're driving."

"The FBI is reopening the case," she said.

Roy didn't say anything as he kept the gun pointed at her and she reached for the car door handle with a trembling hand.

He got into the passenger seat and handed her the keys. "Go to the trailhead of Bear Canyon."

She let out an anguished cry. Now she knew what he had in mind. It was clear why he had grabbed the revolver. He was going to make it look like she had taken her own life in a place that had meant a great deal to her. She and Stewart used to hike Bear Canyon. While they looked down on the valley, they would made plans for their future. Bear Canyon was where Stewart had proposed to her. Given her mother's mental health history, maybe no one would question what had happened.

But Stewart would know. He of all people would know that who your parent was didn't determine who you became. Would there be any evidence to point to who was behind her death? Roy had worn gloves so no fingerprints. He hadn't used a car that could be linked to him. The man was very careful. Would Cindy figure out that something had been put in her tea to knock her out?

"Bear Canyon was the special place for you and Stewart, wasn't it? After you left, he wouldn't stop talking about it like some lovesick puppy."

Tears flowed down Lila's cheeks as she

drove. The road they were on was one where they probably wouldn't encounter any traffic, not on a weekday. She contemplated crashing the car and trying to make a run for it. But it was just too risky. Roy might shoot her on the spot. "Did you kill Stewart's father?" Whatever his answer was, the secret would die with her, but she had to know.

Roy's voice intensified. "The deal between Charlie and me was supposed to be my big break. A chance to use the money to buy a place of my own, so I didn't have to work for a cheat and have nothing to show for it. Stewart Senior found out about it, and he wanted in."

"You killed Stewart's father before you realized the jewels weren't real," she said. "Was what happened to Charlie really an accident?"

"His horse was easy to spook."

She shivered at the realization of how coldhearted and calculating Roy was. He had bided his time to get revenge on everyone who had cheated him. She wanted to ask him why the delay in killing Charlie, but she could guess at the reason. Too many deaths so close together might have raised suspicion. Maybe Charlie had strung him along with the promise of money. Roy had probably intended for the getaway car to be found much sooner if not for the mudslide.

Up ahead, she could see the turnoff for the trailhead. She didn't have much time. Finding out what had happened to Charlie or Stewart's father wasn't the question she most wanted answered.

She stopped the car by the trailhead. He pulled the keys out of the ignition.

"Let me get out first and then you get out real slow." He pushed open the door, keeping the gun aimed at her. When he was standing by her side, he signaled for her to exit the car.

She swiped the tears from her eyes as she exited the car.

"Do you have your phone?"

She nodded.

"Pull it out. You're going to write your suicide note." He stepped closer to her. "And don't try to call for help. I'm watching you."

She pressed on the app that allowed her to write notes to herself. "Please, I have to know. What happened to my father?"

"I feel bad about that. He knew too much."

The stab of pain to her torso left her breathless. Her father was dcad. "But he wasn't in on it, though, was he?"

Roy shook his head. "We needed him to let us into the bank."

"Where is his body?" She had a pretty good idea what the answer to that question was though her mind resisted the reality of her father's death. Roy was wearing a shirt with a missing silver button that looked like the one she had found at the old homestead.

"We've talked enough. Start typing."

The screen in front of her blurred. The gun was still pointed at her. Her throat had gotten so tight, she could barely get out the words. "I don't know what to say."

"Keep it short and sweet. 'I can't take it anymore. It has all been too much.'" He spoke in such a careless way, like her life meant nothing.

She typed with trembling fingers as Roy looked on. Stopping after each word to gaze at the ground around her. There had to be some way she could get away or at least stall.

Her prayer was desperate and unspoken.

Please, God, I don't want to die.

NINETEEN

When Deputy Swain reached the ranch house, Stewart pushed open the car door.

"I'll search the outbuildings," said the deputy as he drew his weapon. Stewart pulled his gun as well and ran inside. His mother looked a bit disoriented when she stepped out of her studio.

"Mom, where is Lila?"

His mother responded slowly. "I don't know. I took a nap on the sofa in my studio. I can't believe how deeply I slept."

The revolver was not on the side table where he'd placed it. "Did you pick up a gun that was here?"

His mom shook her head.

He ran through the house calling Lila's name and then headed toward the kitchen to check the backyard. He scanned the whole area, noticing the tire tracks on the lawn.

Signs of an abduction. Roy's car was parked by the bunkhouse.

Where was she?

He heard voices in the living room. When he returned, his mother stood in front of the open living room door talking to someone he could not see. He hurried across the floor to stand beside his mother. Kurt, the organic farmer, stood on the porch holding a flat of sprouted plants.

"Hey, Stewart," said Kurt. "I was just telling your mom here that I came by to deliver these not more than ten minutes ago, and no one came to the door. I went up the road to make another delivery and thought I would give it another shot on my way back home." He placed the flat of plants in Cindy's hands.

"You were here ten minutes ago? Did you see anything?"

Kurt's expression changed when he locked his gaze on Stewart. He must have seen how worried Stewart was. "Matter of fact there was a blue car just up the road a piece."

"A blue car?"

"Compact, beat-up old piece of junk. The back bumper looked like it was hanging by a thread."

His deputy strode toward them, shaking his head. He ran out to meet his deputy.

"Didn't we have a blue compact car reported stolen earlier? 1980s model from what I remember."

"Yeah, right after you came on shift."

"We need to put out an all-points on it. Last seen on the road by my house."

Both men got into the police car. Stewart got on the radio to notify the Deputy Ridge while Deputy Swain started the car and drove in the direction Stewart had pointed.

There were three possibilities as to where the car might have gone from the road that went past his house, into town, on a road past several farms or into the national forest. He didn't think the culprit would go into town. He notified his other deputy to check for the car in the area where several farms were. He and Deputy Swain headed deeper into the wilderness toward a lake and hiking trails.

His mind raced as his deputy drove. There were dozens of possibilities of where the blue car could have turned off. Plenty of places to hide a body. The one thing he knew for sure was that he didn't have much time.

"We're going to need more help." He got on the radio and notified the forest service.

They passed a sign that indicated how far they were from a picnic area, the trailhead for

Bear Canyon and the lake. The deputy slowed as they approached the picnic area. Stewart couldn't see any sign of a car.

"Should we stop and search the area?" Swain kept his focus on the road.

"No, let's go to the trailhead." Something in his gut told him that they couldn't waste precious minutes stopping to search the first turnout. Maybe it was just because Bear Canyon was such an important part of who he and Lila used to be. Something told him they needed to get there quickly.

Lila's finger hovered over the keypad as she typed the last word of the note that would tell a lie about how she had died.

"Good," said Roy. "Now, hold the phone in your hand and march over there by those trees." He pushed the gun into her back.

If he could touch her with the nose of the gun, he was close. There was a boulder nearby. She took several steps then swung around, knowing she had only one chance to throw him off balance before he could fire a shot at her.

She hit him with her phone then pushed him before turning to run, diving behind the rock just as a bullet glanced off it. Scrambling toward the woods, she headed up the trail, but stayed on it for only a few feet before diving back into the thick of the trees. Another bullet shattered the quiet of the forest.

The terrain grew steeper. Her feet slipped on the loose dirt and leaves. She grabbed a thin tree trunk for support. Though Roy was in good shape from all the physical work he did, she was younger. She might be able to outrun him.

She'd dropped her phone when she hit him with it. Her only choice was to head uphill, but all there was around her was wilderness—no homes, no place to go for help.

The better choice would be to put enough distance between herself and Roy so she could loop back down to the road. She moved as fast as she could.

The hill grew so steep and so precarious that she had to use her hands to climb. She lost her footing and slipped down several feet. Rocks crashed into each other. The noise might have given away her location.

Fatigue set in as she fought to catch her breath. While she anchored one foot against a thin tree, she turned so she had a view of what was downhill. Flashes of movement indicated Roy was still coming up after her.

He came fully into view looking one way and then the other. Her breath caught. He was closer than she realized. Maybe ten yards away.

Her heart pounded as she remained still and prayed he wouldn't notice her. Her clothes were a neutral enough color that they blended in. Trees partially concealed her. The redness in his face indicated that he was as winded as she was.

The seconds ticked by. He stepped off in one direction and then returned to where he had been. He must have sensed that she was close by but hadn't spotted her yet.

Her calf muscle strained as she held herself in place with her foot against the tree trunk.

Roy trudged up the hill with some effort. He was getting closer. She flipped over on her stomach knowing that the noise she made would alert him to her position. But staying here would mean he'd have an easy shot at her once he saw her.

She'd only climbed a few feet when a bullet whizzed through the air. A gasp escaped her lungs, but she kept moving, using her hands to traverse the steep terrain. Rocks tumbled and crashed into each other below her.

"Do you want to know where your father is?"

The question was designed to make her stop and maybe cry out. But she knew the answer. The reason why objects had been moved around at the old homestead trying to cover or hide something. She suspected her father's body was in the well.

She only hoped that secret didn't die with her here in the forest.

TWENTY

Stewart spotted the blue car at the trailhead even before Deputy Swain brought the police vehicle to a full stop. He pushed open the door and jumped out. His deputy got on the radio to advise the other law enforcement that had been called in.

Stewart sprinted toward the trailhead. A phone lay on the ground. He picked it up. Lila's phone. The face of it was cracked.

He headed up the trail. Swain fell in behind him. Stewart hadn't gotten far when he saw a place where the brush had been flattened. Could have been a deer taking off into the forest.

"Split up," he said to Deputy Swain, pointing up the trail. "I'll go this way."

Stewart stepped off the trail looking for more evidence that something or someone had veered off in this direction. A broken tree branch and flattened grass told him which way to go. When he spotted a footprint in some soft earth, he knew that what he was tracking down was human.

A shot splintered the air.

His gut twisted into knots as the silence that proceeded enveloped him. No screams. No follow-up shots.

He moved toward where the shot seemed to have come from knowing that his deputy would have heard the gunfire and would re-route himself to provide backup.

Stewart couldn't wait for help though. Lila might be lying somewhere bleeding out. He kept moving, bending over to climb with his hands, and the mountain became vertical.

A gun was fired in his direction. He pressed his stomach to the ground and lifted his head. No movement. Whoever was up there had the advantage of higher ground.

When Stewart peered down below, he could not see or hear his deputy. The trees blocked much of his view.

He pushed himself up and reached for a rock outcropping for leverage. Climbed several more feet, he stayed as low to the ground as possible. He was able to slip behind a larger rock.

Now when he looked down, he saw Deputy Swain coming toward him, still on the part of the mountain that was flat enough to walk on rather than climb.

As the landscape grew steeper, Swain put away his weapon to maintain his balance. Stewart used hand signals to indicate where the shooter was to his deputy. He nodded in understanding.

Movement in Stewart's peripheral vision caused him to snap his head around. Color flashed between the trees, though he could not see who it was.

Another bullet exploded through the air, but it hadn't come close to him.

Stewart drew his attention down the mountain. His deputy lay on the ground facedown.

"Are you hit?" Stewart called out.

"Yes." It sounded like Deputy Swain was talking through gritted teeth.

"I'm coming down to you."

"No, I'll be all right. Just a flesh wound. You go get him."

Stewart's stomach tied into knots at the tough choice he had to make. Lila was still in danger.

He couldn't see the shooter anywhere. Which meant he had probably decided to go after Lila again.

Stewart headed up the rocky terrain praying he wasn't too late to save Lila and that his deputy would be okay.

He made substantial progress without being shot at. The land leveled off, and he was able to stand upright. Rocks and brush made it hard to see more than a few yards in front of him. The shooter could be hiding anywhere just waiting for him.

He ran from one place of covering to another, stopping to scan for any sign of the shooter or Lila.

As he approached a boulder, he slowed.

A man stepped out from behind the rock. He gripped Lila's arm while he held a gun to her head. Stewart's shock was so complete that he blinked twice before he was willing to see that the man was Roy.

Roy jerked Lila by the arm. "Let me go and she gets to live."

Lila's heart pounded. The cold steel of the gun pressed against her temple.

Even from a distance, the shock on Stewart's face was noticeable. He directed his question at Roy. "Why?"

"Your father cheated me and used me his whole life. Then he stole the one chance I had of getting a ranch of my own."

Stewart shook his head in disbelief. He

lowered the gun a few inches. "But I didn't. I kept you on. Paid you a fair wage."

"Some things you just can't undo," said Roy. "Enough talk. You let me go and I won't shoot her. Put your gun on the ground and your hands in the air."

Stewart's posture softened. The confident lawman stance that he took on when he was on duty disappeared. It was clear that finding out a man he had worked beside for all these years was a killer had sent him into a tailspin.

"Let her go," he said.

"Drop the gun first." Roy tightened his grip on Lila's arm causing pain to shoot up to her shoulder.

Lila's whole body shook. This man had killed at least four times. He would have no qualms about shooting her. Yet that killing had been done when there were no witnesses. She had the terrible feeling that neither she nor Stewart were going to leave here alive.

"Don't do it, Stewart." Her voice filled with anguish and fear. Could Stewart bring himself to shoot Roy?

"I said drop the gun." Roy edged closer to her, jabbing the gun at her temple.

Stewart stared at his gun for a long moment and then at Roy. He dropped the gun to the ground.

Roy pushed Lila toward Stewart so she crashed against him, and they fell on the ground.

To her surprise, Roy did not shoot at them. He took off running toward the thick of the trees. Maybe he did have a conscience that he couldn't bring himself to shoot a man who had been fair to him, not while he faced him anyway.

After scooping up his gun, Stewart took off running. "I have to get him. You stay put."

He ran only a short distance before stopping and returning to Lila. "I think I lost him. I don't know what's on the other side of this canyon."

"I don't know either. It's not part of the trail we hiked."

Stewart stopped to talk into his radio. "Swain, how are you doing?"

"Hanging in there. Help should be here any minute."

"We're going to have to set up a search for a fugitive." Stewart took in a raspy breath. "His name is… Roy Valentine."

The deputy didn't answer right away. "Really? Where was he last seen?"

"Headed up the canyon on foot," said Stewart. "Forest Service will know better the possible places Roy might decide to escape to or hide."

Now that he could be identified, he wasn't going to stick around. Lila's knees felt like they might buckle.

Stewart gathered Lila into a sideways hug. "Let's head back down. I've got a deputy that needs medical attention."

"You must feel horribly betrayed."

"I've been paying my father's bills so to speak for a long time. I won't lie to you. This one really hurts."

They hiked and half crawled down the steep part of the mountain. Once they were on the trail, they made quick progress. When they stepped free of the trees, the sun was low in the cloudy sky. Two cars with the Forest Service insignia on them along with an ambulance and the other sheriff's vehicle filled up the small gravel parking lot. The deputy had already been loaded into the ambulance. Stewart ran to check on him and then gather the other law enforcement into a huddle before breaking and walking over to Lila.

"Come on, I'll take you back to the ranch house. We have a long night ahead of us," said Stewart.

There wasn't much of a chance to talk on the way back. Radio calls came in from the other law enforcement people as to where they were looking.

She didn't mind the lack of conversation. She felt overwhelmed by what she had learned. Her father was dead but innocent of involvement in the robbery.

An officer's voice came through the radio. "We just had a report of a stolen car at a turnout not too far from the trailhead. We believe the suspect looped down the mountain and took it."

Stewart spoke into the radio. "Description of the vehicle?"

"A tan short-bed pickup."

"Direction of travel?"

"Believed to be headed north."

"Stay in touch. I intend to remain with Lila while our perp is still at large." Stewart parked the car in front of the ranch house.

She turned to face him. "My father is dead. He was coerced into opening the bank, probably at gunpoint."

"Roy told you that?"

"In so many words," Lila said. "I think I know where his body is. The reason why there were lights the first time by the old homestead was because Roy was probably trying to see if he could remove the body.

The second time I think he just tried to cover it up better."

Stewart shook his head, not understanding.

"I think my father's body is down that old well. I'm want to see. I have to know."

"I don't want you out there alone. We can get flashlights and raincoats from the house."

By the time they had located the flashlights and stepped out on the porch, the rain was coming down in sheets.

"Why don't we wait this out?" He looked up at the sky. "It should let up in a few minutes. I'll feel better about going out there once Roy is in custody."

They sat on the wicker couch watching and listening to the rain. Lila had always thought the rain sounded like nature's symphony. The silence between them felt comfortable. They both had a lot to process.

Stewart's radio made a fizzy noise and a voice came through. "We have a visual on the truck. Suspect should be in custody shortly."

"Ten-four."

Lila relaxed. This whole ordeal would be over soon.

Within minutes, the downpour turned into a drizzle, and they headed toward the old homestead.

Lila hoped that she was right about where

her father's body was. Once Roy was in custody and her house on the market, she could close this chapter of her life and get back to Seattle.

Stewart parked the car as close as he could get to the old homestead. Lila pushed open the door and ran toward the well. She was already shining her flashlight down it when he caught up with her.

"I see the logs that must have been picked up and tossed down there," she said. "I can't see much else. It's really dark."

He pulled his flashlight out and moved to the other side of the well. The overgrown trees and dark sky didn't make it any easier to discover if Lila's theory was correct. Leaning over as far as he dared, he clicked on his light and angled it to try to cover the areas that Lila's light didn't reach.

Lila rested her stomach against the rim of the well so she could illuminate more of it.

He saw now that more debris besides the logs had been thrown down the well, including pieces of plywood and what looked like part of an appliance.

Lila moved her flashlight inch by inch. She gasped. "There."

He looked where her light was pointing.

Though it was barely discernible he was pretty sure he was staring at several finger bones. "We'll get the crime scene people out here and get an ID."

He wondered how Lila would deal with the news. She finally had her answer, but it wasn't a good one.

He was just about to straighten his back to ask her how she was feeling when a voice came through the radio.

"Found the truck not too far from your place. Suspect has escaped on foot."

Stewart straightened up just in time to see a hand wrap around Lila's neck and yank her backward. Lila didn't even have time to cry out before the gun was pointed at her stomach.

He looked into Roy's eyes.

"Your father stole my dream from me. What if I take something you love from you?"

Stewart knew if he reached for his gun it would be over for Lila.

"That's not justice, that's revenge."

"You do love her, don't you?"

The rain pattered on his hat. "Yes."

Lila let out a gasp as she kept her gaze on Stewart.

Roy's eyes were glassy and unfocused. Stewart was looking at a desperate man who knew it was over for him. "You don't want to do this, Roy."

"I want some justice too. Some fairness." The bravado had left the other man's voice.

"Let her go."

Roy's lip quivered, and then he pushed Lila toward Stewart and lifted the gun. Stewart stepped between the two people, holding his hands in the air. "Haven't you exacted enough revenge on both our families and Mrs. Inman?"

"I was betrayed." Roy aimed the gun at him and pulled back the hammer on the revolver Stewart had meant for Lila to use for protection. Roy must have taken it.

"Put the gun down." Though his heart pounded intensely, he managed to keep his voice authoritative, not giving away the level of fear coursing through his body. His tone softened. "You don't want to do this."

Roy's hand went limp, and he dropped the gun on the ground. When Stewart moved in to handcuff him, Roy did not resist.

Stewart heard sirens in the distance. As he led the man who had betrayed him, a man he had trusted, toward the police vehicle, he realized nothing in life was certain other than the faithfulness of God.

TWENTY ONE

Lila stood at the graveside of her father's new tombstone. The body in the well had been identified, and she was able to arrange a long overdue funeral for her father. She was grateful to see that many people from town, including Mrs. Inman, had shown up. Stewart, his brother and mother had come as well.

The last few weeks had been a whirlwind of trying to get the house ready to put on the market and arranging for her father to have a proper burial. Even though Stewart came to help her with the packing and moving anytime she asked, their conversations had been around safe subjects.

When he'd thought she might die, he had confessed to loving her. Had he meant it? Or was it a confession induced by the danger and intensity of the moment? Even if he did love her, she didn't know what she felt about him. All the trauma and tragedy made it hard to even sort through her feelings. Had the attraction been driven by her need to be close to the man she knew would protect her? Or was it really love?

She'd prayed about it and asked God to give her some clarity. Otherwise she would go through with the sale of the house and return to Seattle.

She was alone now by her father's grave. While the others had left for the potluck at the church, she had stayed behind to have a private moment. She laid the bouquet of daisies she'd been holding on top of the fresh grave and stood up. "I miss you, Daddy. I love you."

She turned to go when she saw Stewart coming toward her from the edge of the graveyard. He stopped several feet away and took off his cowboy hat. "Elliot and Mom went on ahead. I thought I could drive you to the church."

"Sure. I'd like that."

They walked across the grounds toward the road where her rental car was parked.

He grabbed her arm, and she turned to look at him. "I think I should say this now before things get busy and people are around. I'm going to miss you."

She looked into his eyes and saw angst

there. "I'm going to miss you too. I appreciate everything you've done to help me. You know what I am going to miss more than anything?"

"What?"

"I miss who we could have been together before the robbery. It would have been a beautiful life."

"The people we were when we were eighteen don't exist anymore. The man I was before I found out what Roy had done to my father and yours doesn't exist anymore."

"What are you saying?"

"I'm saying that tragedy and trials change a person. We can't go back in time. We fell out of love because of everything that happened. The time I have been able to spend with you made me realize that I love the person you are now."

Lila's throat went dry. She licked her lips. "You meant it when you said you loved me?"

He reached up to rest his hand on her face. "We are both older and wiser now, not naive about how the world is. I think we're strong enough to weather the inevitable storms of life. I'd like for us to do that together."

"You want me to stay in Trident?"

"Yes, to stay and to be my wife. Lila, will you marry me?"

She knew what her answer was as she gazed into his eyes. They were different people to each other than they had been ten years ago. And she loved the man Stewart had become. "What we have together is not an innocent first love. It's brand-new and so much deeper than that." She rested her hand on his chest where she could feel his heart beating as her gaze found his. "Yes, Stewart, I will marry you."

He gathered her into his arms and kissed her.

* * * * *

If you enjoyed this story, look for these other books by Sharon Dunn:

Christmas Hostage
Crime Scene Cover-Up

Dear Reader,

I hope you enjoyed the excitement of not only the danger Lila and Stewart faced but the journey they went on to fall in love again with each other. As I was writing this book, I thought a great deal about what it means to live in a small town for generations and to have everyone be aware of your family history. In Montana where I grew up and now live, that can be a good and bad thing. Both Lila and Stewart have a shadow cast over their lives because of who their parents were. Stewart is driven to prove that, unlike his father, he is an honest man. Lila worries that people assume she will suffer from the same mental illness struggles as her mother. While there are so many wonderful things about small towns, people assuming that *the acorn doesn't fall far from the tree* isn't one of them. One of the neatest things about this book is that both Lila and Stewart are able to forge identities separate from who their parents were, and it aids in them being able to commit to and love each other for a second time in a more mature way. How about you?

Everyone has some shadow on their lives based on something another relative has done. How did you step free of that?

Blessings on you,
Sharon Dunn